KHANDAV

A Horror Sci-Fi Journey Into the
Depths of Myth and Madness

Mahesh Rajmane

notionpress.com

INDIA • SINGAPORE • MALAYSIA

ISBN
Paperback 979-8-89724-587-1
Hardcase 979-8-89744-608-7

For my family,

who gave me the space to dream and the strength to create,

even when it meant I couldn't always be present.

Contents

The Jungle's Embrace

– Alice's Adventures in Wonderland

The world is fair in that it is unfair to everyone. To the snail inching up a tree, its path a perfect, innocent straight line, blissfully unaware of the predator above. To the laborers sleeping on the roadside, their faces softened by dreams of tomorrow's meal, crushed beneath the wheels of a rich man's speeding car before morning ever came. To the Bollywood actress, rehearsing her speech for the award she was destined to win, slipping in her bathtub, her skull meeting porcelain, and breaking the hearts of millions with her untimely end. Fairness, it seemed, lay in the impartial cruelty woven into the fabric of life itself—a design indifferent to innocence or intent.

And it was fair to Maruti Pawar. Fair in its mercilessness, fair in the way it had burdened him with a melancholy so profound it felt like an anchor, pulling him into an abyss he couldn't escape.

His face was pale, his eyes hollow. A man consumed by despair. In the silence of his mud hut, he sought relief from the relentless anguish that had settled like a parasite in his mind. Thoughts of suicide had become his familiar companions, whispering promises of peace. He had imagined every way— pesticides, cliffs, ropes.

The noose, though, held a strange, haunting allure. There was somber poetry in it: a lifeless body swaying from a rope, defying the laws of nature. Animals didn't hang from ropes. This macabre ritual was reserved for humans—a deliberate end, a final act of defiance.

His empty gaze wandered across the hut, lingering on the cracked clay walls that had borne witness to his silent battles. Shadows from the flickering kerosene lamp danced across the room, shifting shapes in the dim light as if mocking him. A single, worn blanket lay crumpled in the corner—the same blanket that had shielded him through countless winters, though it seemed to offer little warmth now. Every object in the room seemed to stare back at him, bearing silent testimony to nights of isolation and dreams that had crumbled like the parched earth outside.

"How did it come to this?" Maruti whispered into the void, his voice trembling with disbelief. He had always been a good man—hadn't he? Even through the twists and turns of life, through the fleeting triumphs and the crushing descents, he held on to his goodness. Yet, this was where he stood now, staring into the abyss. Was this all a good man deserved?

The universe, careless and indifferent, had chewed him up and spat him out, mocking his morality with every blow it dealt. He had been loved once—truly loved. He had parents who cherished him, neighbors who smiled at him like he was one of their own. He had friends who laughed with him, shared his joys, his pains. It had all seemed so permanent. Solid. But it wasn't.

"What happened?" he muttered, the question lingering like smoke in the cold air. Was it the drinks? A small, bitter laugh escaped his lips. No, the drinks were just a symptom, not the disease. The disease was life itself—a cruel joke, a rigged game where the only certainty was loss.

With a heavy sigh, he slung the rope over his shoulder. In his other hand, he held a half-empty bottle of alcohol—his refuge and tormentor. The glass was warm against his palm, a fleeting comfort that dulled his pain, though never for long.

Outside, the air was still, heavy with the scent of dust and dry grass. As he stepped toward the door, he cast one last, lingering look around his hut, as if hoping it might offer him a reason to stay. But the walls remained silent, as they always had.

"Farewell, Dongarwadi," he whispered, the words barely audible. This place had seen him at his lowest, had absorbed his loneliness, his anger, his regrets. Now, he left it behind, stepping into the unknown.

Dongarwadi was a quiet village, nestled on the border between Maharashtra and Karnataka. Surrounded by nature's bounty, it lay hidden along a sinuous black road that meandered through dense forests—a path known only to those who dared to venture beyond the reach of city lights. Life here unfolded slowly, like the steady rhythm of a heart untroubled by the ticking of a clock. Shielded from the grasp of modern technology, mobile networks and the pervasive presence of the Internet were but distant whispers, unable to pierce the sanctuary of this secluded realm.

In this timeless enclave, a single telephone line, housed within the neglected post office, served as the village's tenuous connection to the outside world. Dongarwadi was like a forgotten chapter, waiting to be closed. The youth, once the vibrant heartbeat of the village, had fled to distant cities, chasing the neon glow of modernity and leaving behind fading memories and aging parents.

At the heart of the village stood an ancient Peepal tree, its thick, gnarled branches stretching high into the sky. No one in Dongarwadi had ever seen it small, not even Ramu Savarde, who was now nearing eighty. For as long as anyone could remember, the tree had loomed over the village like a silent guardian, its vast, sprawling canopy casting a protective shadow over everything beneath it. The villagers revered the tree as a living ancestor, a symbol of enduring strength. Legends whispered that it had stood for over five centuries, long before the village had taken shape around it. Its roots, thick as a man's arm, seemed to reach deep into the earth, anchoring Dongarwadi to its storied past.

Beneath this ancient sentinel stood a modest Hanuman temple, its small stone structure nestled at the base of the Peepal's trunk, as though shielded by the tree's vast limbs. The temple, simple yet dignified, bore faded garlands and streaks of red sindoor smeared across its stones—a humble homage to the deity watching over Dongarwadi.

Each year, the Peepal tree and the temple became the heart of a vibrant tapestry of devotion. Colorful prayer flags fluttered in the breeze, tied high on the branches, while delicate threads bound the villagers' hopes and prayers to the tree's ancient limbs. Together, the temple and the tree stood as silent witnesses to the rhythms of life in Dongarwadi, symbols of stability and spirituality in a world slowly slipping away.

Ramchandra Savarde, a weathered old farmer, sat beneath the sprawling shade of the Peepal tree, his wrinkled hands resting on his cane as he watched the village with eyes that had seen generations come and go. A short distance away, a young woman scrubbed utensils in front of her house, drawing the attention of a group of middle-aged men standing on the road, like moths to a flame. Her back was straight, her posture confident. Her blouse clung to her form, and with each movement, her cleavage became visible—a tantalizing curve that seemed to deepen with every shift. Her motions accentuated the gentle rise and fall of her chest, the swell of her breasts catching the light in a way that held the men captive.

Each turn of her body, each deliberate gesture, seemed to invite their gaze. The rhythm of her movements created a mesmerizing effect. She was aware of their attention—her eyes flicked up occasionally, a knowing glint flashing within them— but she kept her gaze averted, her mouth set in a slight, enigmatic smile. To the men, her confidence only heightened her allure. The sway of her hips as she shifted, the subtle bounce with every motion, created a silent yet unmistakable invitation.

Ramu's gaze hardened as he noticed the men's fixation. In his youth, such blatant behavior would have been unheard of; respectability was the hallmark of a woman's character. But the young woman seemed indifferent to his silent judgment, her eyes focused on her task, her hands moving rhythmically over the utensils. She avoided his gaze, but Ramu could sense her defiance—a quiet power that neither the ancient tree's watchfulness nor his disapproving stare could diminish.

The men stood transfixed, caught in her quiet spell. Their idle chatter faded into silence, the air thick with unspoken tension. It was a mingling of the sacred and the earthly, as if the Peepal tree itself observed this small human drama with an age-old wisdom that transcended judgment.

"Hey, you pathetic cuck!" one of the men jeered, his voice dripping with contempt as Maruti emerged from the shadowed alleyway. He cut a figure of both strength and despair, his once-toned frame now marred by grime. His dirty, sleeveless banyan clung to his wiry physique, and his torn jeans whispered of a life in tatters. Slung over his shoulder was a haunting coil of rope, while his hands clutched the bottle of cheap alcohol that had become his only companion.

The villagers, long accustomed to his tortured existence, seemed to take pleasure in tormenting him. They called him 'Cuckold'—a cruel echo of his past. Maruti had once commanded respect in the village, earning an honest living as a driver in a neighboring town. His marriage to the beautiful Laxmi had been the envy of many, her laughter filling their humble home with warmth and light. For a time, it seemed as though he had everything a man could ask for.

But life has a way of unraveling even the strongest threads. Poverty, coupled with his growing reliance on alcohol, began to strain their union. Or perhaps, it hadn't been entirely his fault. Perhaps he had been deliberately pushed toward ruin—subtly, cruelly—by scheming men with jealous hearts and lustful eyes. Men who envied him for having her, for holding something they could never possess. Their poisoned whispers crept into his life like a slow venom, steering him toward the bottle and the gambling den. They didn't need to destroy him outright; they simply nudged him closer to the precipice, watching as he stumbled into the abyss of his own despair.

And then there was Laxmi. The village's so-called "respectable" men had seduced her, weaving a web of deceit around her until she no longer looked at Maruti with the same love. He, blinded by devotion, had ignored the signs, dismissing the rumors that reached his ears. Until the day she vanished. She left with a passing truck driver, taking with her not just her belongings, but also his dreams and what was left of his fragile heart.

Maruti's drinking, which had already taken root in his life, worsened in the wake of her betrayal. What had once been a vice he could manage spiraled into an all-consuming addiction. He sought solace at the bottom of every bottle, drowning his anguish day after day. The habit quickly devoured his life. It cost him his job, his dignity, and the respect he had once held in the community. Reduced to a hollow shell of his former self, he scraped by with menial tasks, trading his pride for a few coins or a sip of rum.

Now, the villagers' jeers cut through him like a blade, their laughter echoing in his ears as a relentless reminder of all he had lost.

"Cuck!" sneered another man, relishing his misery. Nearby, the woman scrubbing dishes twisted her lips into a cruel smile, her amusement unspoken but evident. "Maybe he's searching for Laxmi," someone else mocked, their words biting and dripping with derision.

The weight of their cruelty pressed down on him. "I'm going to die," Maruti declared suddenly, his voice raw with intensity. His words hung in the air, met only with laughter and scorn. The villagers were merciless.

"You bastards!" he roared, his voice fueled by a sudden burst of rage. "I'll haunt this village. I curse every one of you. I curse this wretched place!" His fury rang out, but it fell on deaf ears. The villagers laughed harder, their cruel mirth echoing through the air.

Only Ramu, sitting beneath the Peepal tree, broke the cycle of mockery. "Why do you torment him?" he shouted, his voice cutting through their laughter. "Can't you see he's at his breaking point? Have you no shame? Leave him alone!"

His furious gaze landed on the woman washing dishes, an unspoken condemnation in his eyes. Reluctantly, the group dispersed, their laughter fading into the distance.

"Cuck is sad!" one of them called out mockingly. "With the loss of Laxmi, the whole village is sad," another added, their voices trailing off with cruel giggles.

Maruti stood still, his gaze following their retreating figures. His eyes, devoid of interest, flicked briefly to the woman, whose seductive allure held no power over him. Taking two desperate swigs from the bottle, he turned his attention to the ancient Peepal tree. The tree had long been his refuge, its steadfast presence a silent companion through the trials of his childhood. It was a living relic in a desolate village, a keeper of his most cherished memories.

As he gazed up at its gnarled branches, memories flooded his mind, their roots intertwining with the tree's ancient limbs.

He could almost hear his mother's voice, tender yet concerned, calling out to him as he scaled those branches in his youth. But now, as he stood beneath the towering sentinel, an unsettling chill crept through his veins. The tree's silence felt alive, its presence charged with an intensity that sent shivers down his spine. Was it his imagination, or did the tree hold the answers he desperately sought?

"They drove my Laxmi away," he whispered into the stillness. "The whole cursed village tormented her..." His heartache spilled into the quiet, his words carried to the tree as if it could offer solace or understanding.

The tree stood stoic, its ancient bark seeming to absorb his grief. Its roots anchored him to memories he could never escape. For a fleeting moment, he thought he saw its branches shift slightly, as though reaching out to him in silent empathy.

With a heart heavy with sorrow, Maruti reluctantly tore himself away from the tree's embrace. Ramu's concerned gaze followed him, an unspoken understanding passing between them as Maruti walked away, his footsteps weighed down by the burdens of his past and the inevitable end that awaited him.

The woman gathered her utensils and retreated into her house. Ramu remained beneath the tree, watching Maruti's figure disappear into the distance. He muttered softly, his voice laced with concern, "Mother Chendkai, please help him."

Leaving the village behind, Maruti trudged onto the road that wound toward the looming mountain. Each step felt heavier, burdened by the torment of his memories. The bottle in his hand had lost its numbing power; only a hollow rage and bitter despair drove him forward.

As he walked, his eyes caught sight of a lone man relieving himself in the bushes, a bicycle propped idly against the road. Without hesitation, Maruti seized the moment. He leapt onto the bicycle and pedaled away with reckless abandon. Behind him, the startled man turned sharply, splashing his own legs in shock. "Stop, you drunken fool! You miserable excuse for a man!" the man bellowed, his curses swallowed by the wind as Maruti disappeared down the road. He made a half-hearted attempt to give chase but soon gave up, resigned to wait for a passing motorbike.

Maruti pedaled furiously, his rage and desperation propelling him through the dense jungle. The foliage grew thicker with each turn, and the paved road dissolved into a treacherous, muddy path. A weathered signpost loomed ahead, its message scrawled in dripping red paint: "KHANDAV." Beneath the name, an ominous skull and crossed bones were painted, a silent but unmistakable warning. The arrow beneath pointed toward a murky path that twisted into the depths of the jungle.

Behind him, the roar of a motorcycle engine grew louder. "Catch that fool!" a voice shouted, the words riding the wind. His pursuers had arrived, intent on catching him. Without hesitation, Maruti abandoned the bicycle, letting it crash into the undergrowth, and sprinted down the muddy trail. His breath came in ragged gasps, his heart pounding as he plunged deeper into the unknown.

Suddenly, he froze. Ahead of him stood a small, peculiar statue—no more than three feet tall. Carved from black stone, it depicted a naked goddess. Her body was adorned with vivid smears of red kumkum and yellow turmeric powder, the colors lending her both reverence and menace. In one hand, she held a stone machete, its edge chipped yet fierce, a symbol of her power. Her other hand was raised in a warning, her posture exuding both protection and foreboding. She was Mother Chendkai, the guardian of Khandav, a divine sentinel of the jungle's untamed depths.

Maruti's breath caught in his throat. Fear and awe coursed through him as he stared at the idol. For a fleeting moment, the weight of the village's superstitions pressed down on him—the fear of spirits, curses, and unseen forces. But his rage burned hotter than his fear. No statue, no goddess, could stop him now. With a final glance at the idol, he turned and leapt into the foliage, disappearing like a shadow into the jungle's embrace.

The motorcycle screeched to a halt near the discarded bicycle. "You goddamn bastard!" one of the men snarled, glaring at the muddy path ahead. Both men dismounted, their eyes scanning the dark trail where Maruti had vanished. They had planned to teach him a harsh lesson—but now, their anger wavered. The name "Khandav" loomed in their minds, a place of dread that even their bravado could not conquer.

"Stop, Maruti! Don't go in there!" the man whose bicycle had been stolen shouted, his voice trembling with desperation.

"Damn it... he's crossed the goddess," the other muttered, disbelief lacing his tone.

Their eyes met, uncertainty flickering in their eyes. "Should we follow him?" the second man asked, his voice trembling with hesitation.

"Are you mad?" the first man snapped. "No one defies Mother Chendkai. No one! You've heard the stories—those who enter Khandav don't come back."

"But this is just the replica... right?" the second man countered, desperation creeping into his tone. "The real one's deep in the jungle!"

The first man scowled, lowering his voice as if even speaking about it could draw her ire. "No one sees the real one and lives to tell about it. Except maybe Bhairav..." His gaze darted toward the dense shadows of the forest. "They say she's massive, ancient—been watching over this jungle long before we existed."

The statue at the edge of the jungle was no ancient relic. It had been erected only a few years ago, a smaller, humbler replica of the true Chendkai statue hidden deep within the forest. But it had served its purpose. Fear, after all, was stronger than any law. Those who were superstitious didn't question it; they didn't need to. The stories, the whispers, the disappearances—all of it had woven a spell stronger than reason. The replica stood as both a warning and a silent barrier, keeping most of the villagers from ever stepping beyond the jungle's threshold.

They both turned to the looming shadows of the jungle. A heavy silence settled between them, the air thick and oppressive. Finally, the first man stepped forward, bowing his head toward the smaller idol. "May Mother Chendkai show mercy on his tormented soul," he murmured.

His companion hesitated, then followed suit, their silent prayers carried by the thick, humid air as the jungle seemed to shiver with life, swallowing Maruti whole.

Without another word, they turned back. One man climbed onto the motorcycle, while the other mounted the bicycle, steadying himself by gripping the biker's shoulder. Slowly, they began their retreat to the village, careful not to look back at the cursed road leading into Khandav. The jungle, vast and foreboding, swallowed the path ahead like a beast awaiting its next victim.

Drenched in sweat from his desperate journey, Maruti had trekked through the jungle for hours before finding himself beneath a towering tree. The eerie beauty of the wilderness pressed in on him, and a creeping dread began to settle in his chest. To ward off his fear, he began to sing, his voice slicing through the oppressive silence. "*Zindagi khwab hai...*" he crooned, the melancholy tune echoing through the jungle.

He scanned the dense forest around him before climbing the tree, settling on a sturdy branch. Humming softly, he tied the rope to a small offshoot, fashioning a crude noose. His eyes wandered over the jungle one last time, as if bidding the world farewell. But in his moment of despair, his balance faltered. With a sickening thud, his body hit the ground, pain shooting through his limbs.

Through gritted teeth, Maruti cursed and resumed his song, the haunting melody a stubborn defiance against his own failures. Above him, the noose swung mockingly, just out of reach. He retrieved a bottle from his pocket and sighed in relief to find it intact. Kissing it tenderly, he climbed the tree once more.

Perched on the branch again, Maruti slipped the noose around his neck and sighed heavily. Draining the last of the rum, he poured a few drops onto the tree. "You deserve a drink too," he muttered. "I wonder how you've stood here for decades." He kissed the branch, then tossed the empty bottle to the ground below, where it shattered with a hollow crack.

The alcohol coursed through his veins, its numbing warmth overtaking him. Slumping against the branch, he whispered a drunken confession. "Laxmi, I'll become a ghost and haunt you. I know you love me... that truck driver... he hypnotized you..." His words trailed off, and he drifted into a restless slumber.

The sun dipped below the horizon, and the jungle embraced the encroaching darkness. Silence reigned, broken only by the chirping of crickets and Maruti's soft snores.

As his dreams deepened, they turned to nightmares.

He stood before a massive tree, its shadowy branches clawing at the sky. Beneath it, a truck idled, its cabin lights casting an eerie glow under the full moon. Maruti peered inside, his heart pounding. Laxmi lay sprawled across the seat, her body writhing beneath the truck driver. Her moans filled the still night as the driver moved relentlessly, his face hidden in shadow.

Maruti stood frozen, helpless, as her body arched and twisted in pleasure. Then, suddenly, she turned her gaze toward him, her eyes wide and glinting with desire. "Maruti, you came! I love you!" she cried, her voice dripping with ecstasy even as her body remained captive to the driver's rhythm.

The driver turned slowly—too slowly. His head twisted a full 180 degrees, revealing a devilish face with glowing red eyes and a grotesque, lolling tongue. Inhuman sounds rumbled from his throat, deep and guttural, reverberating in the night air.

Fear gripped Maruti, his chest tight as his breath came in short, panicked bursts. He stared into the glowing eyes of the beast, his body paralyzed by terror.

The nightmare broke abruptly. Maruti jolted awake, his body convulsing as panic seized him. In his frantic movements, he lost his balance, slipping off the branch. The noose tightened around his neck, leaving his legs dangling inches above the ground.

With desperate, ragged gasps, Maruti clawed at the rope, trying to pull himself up. But the alcohol had dulled his strength, and the noose bit into his skin. His legs kicked violently, thrashing against the inevitability of death.

Then, the ground beneath him began to stir.

The mud and leaves shifted, moving in a spectral breeze. The earth itself seemed to rise, taking shape, until it formed the towering figure of a goddess. Standing ten feet tall, her dusky stone body exuded both power and foreboding. She fixed Maruti with an unyielding gaze, her presence filling the air with a primal energy.

Maruti's breath hitched, his voice a faint rasp. "Mother Chendkai..." he managed to whisper.

The goddess stepped forward, her movements slow and deliberate. Her voice, deep and thunderous, echoed through the jungle. "Why have you come? Flee, foolish mortal! Begone!"

At her command, a loud snap resounded through the air. The branch to which the noose was tied broke, sending Maruti crashing to the ground. His legs touched the earth, but his strength failed him, and he collapsed in a lifeless heap.

The jungle returned to its stillness. No goddess remained. The tree stood silent, its ancient limbs unmoving, as though nothing had happened.

Had the branch snapped first, birthing the hallucination of the deity in Maruti's mind? Or had the goddess truly intervened, severing the rope at her will? Like when you fall off a cliff in a dream, only to wake up just in time, teetering at the edge of your bed. Coincidence? A forewarning glimpsed in sleep? Or just a false memory stitched together by the mind upon waking? The answer lay beyond comprehension, obscured by the depths of the jungle and the mysteries of Khandav.

Maruti lay unconscious for another hour, his body sprawled beneath the towering tree. The jungle watched in silence, its secrets untouched by human understanding.

Maruti lay motionless, vulnerable, as a gentle, feminine hand brushed against his cracked lips. His eyes fluttered open, and there she was—Laxmi. Draped in a flowing white saree, her beauty seemed almost otherworldly. The ethereal fabric clung to her form, hinting at the curves beneath, her allure both delicate and powerful. She laughed softly, her gaze locking with his, a silent invitation to follow.

He reached out, desperate to grasp her hand, but she slipped away with a teasing laugh, her figure retreating into the shadows. Her ample hips swayed seductively, her movements both enticing and surreal, as though the jungle itself bent to her presence.

"Laxmi!" Maruti called, scrambling to his feet, the rope and broken offshoot branch trailing behind him.

She moved effortlessly through the dense jungle, her form gliding at times, floating without visible steps, and at others, vanishing only to reappear behind towering trees. Her gaze beckoned him, daring him to follow. Maruti stumbled after her, driven by a potent mix of longing and obsession.

The trailing branch snagged on low-hanging foliage, pulling him to the ground. Cursing under his breath, he tore the rope from his neck, untangling himself before staggering to his feet once more. He couldn't lose her—not now.

The wind carried strange melodies, whispering through the trees, while the leaves seemed to shimmer and dance in her wake. She led him deeper into the heart of the jungle, her silhouette framed against the shadowed embrace of a colossal tree. Its roots spread wide like a throne, and there, at its center, she settled. Leaning back against the ancient trunk, her eyes burned into his with an intensity that pulled him inescapably closer.

Maruti rushed to her, tripping over exposed roots as he collapsed at her feet. His lips brushed her bare toes, trembling as he surrendered to her presence. Laxmi bent down gracefully, her hands cradling his head with a tenderness that felt divine. Slowly, seductively, she pulled him closer, and her warm lips met his.

Tears rolled down Maruti's cheeks as a strange warmth engulfed him. For the first time in what felt like an eternity, he felt whole.

But then, Laxmi began to change.

The radiant beauty of her face withered, her smooth skin peeling and shriveling like paper left too long in the sun. Her saree, once pristine and elegant, rotted away in strips, exposing her decayed form beneath. The soft hand that had cradled his face turned skeletal, its bony fingers wrapped with crawling vines.

The figure before him, pressed against the massive tree, was no longer human. Roots and tendrils coiled tightly around her desiccated frame, binding her to the tree as though nature itself had claimed her. Mushrooms sprouted grotesquely from her eye sockets, their swollen caps pulsating faintly with an eerie light. The hollow cavities of her skull gaped at Maruti, the mushrooms pushing through bone and jaw like parasitic invaders.

A GoPro, still clinging to the remains of the skull, was half-buried in moss and strangled by vines. Its cracked lens, smeared with decay, seemed to stare back at him, a silent witness to whatever horror had unfolded.

The air around them thickened with shimmering particles, glowing faintly as if alive with decay. They clung to the tatters of her saree, making the rotting fabric shimmer with a sickly, moldy glow.

The vines wrapped tighter around the skeletal figure, merging it with the colossal tree. The once-human form now seemed like an offering consumed by the jungle itself. The grotesque mockery of life exuded a presence that was both horrifying and mesmerizing, as though the jungle breathed in time with the twisted remains.

Maruti knelt before her, lost in his trance, oblivious to the decay seeping through his illusion. To him, she was still Laxmi—warm, alive, and whole. Her presence was overwhelming, her lips soft against his. As their mouths met, he felt her saliva—sweet and intoxicating—spreading across his tongue. Yet, beneath the veil of his mind, the forest grew restless. The air thickened with a sickly-sweet stench.

A damp squelch broke the silence, jarring him. He froze, his lips brushing something cold and spongy. The mushroom burst, splattering his face with its rancid, oozing liquid. The taste turned bitter and foul, the illusion shattering as the reality of the decay seeped into his senses.

Yet, Maruti didn't recoil. He didn't gag or flinch. The delusion held him in its grip, and even as the putrid liquid soaked his skin and filled his senses, he remained motionless.

In his mind, he was still kissing Laxmi, still lost in her embrace, blind to the macabre nightmare that surrounded him.

The Missing Botanist

"I am a cage, in search of a bird."

– Franz Kafka

The café, a small retreat at the edge of a bustling road, offered a surprising oasis of calm amidst the chaos. Outside, the honking of cars and the rush of pedestrians painted a picture of unrelenting motion, but inside, the world seemed to pause. Conversations hummed softly, the occasional clatter of cups punctuating the air. In the corner, a couple sat close, their fingers intertwined, whispering over their coffee as if the world beyond didn't exist.

Maya Bhosle, sitting by the window, exhaled deeply as she stirred her coffee. In her early thirties, she carried an effortless charm, though it often felt like a fragile mask these days. Her brown skin glowed faintly under the soft light, her sharp features etched with a quiet resilience that bordered on defiance. Her short, cropped hair framed her face, adding a touch of modernity to her otherwise classic beauty. She wore fitted jeans with frayed hems and a snug T-shirt, layered with an unbuttoned shirt that swayed gently as she shifted in her seat. It was a look crafted not just for comfort but as armor—an attempt to cling to her identity amidst an indifferent world.

She glanced briefly at the couple in the corner, a pang of something raw tugging at her as Sonia's words echoed in her mind.

"Don't worry, Sonia. I'll return the money by next month. I promise," Maya had said, her voice low but pleading.

Sonia, her best friend and a pragmatist to the core, raised an eyebrow, her skepticism sharp. "You said that last month, Maya."

Maya bit her lip. "But you're my best friend!"

Sonia sighed, leaning back in her chair. Her gaze softened for a moment before flickering to the couple holding hands. Then she turned back to Maya. "Maya, how much longer can you go on like this? You need a job."

"If only I could find one," Maya muttered, frustration seeping into her voice. Her eyes darted to the couple again, envy creeping into her thoughts. Why did life seem so easy for some people?

Sonia studied her carefully. "There's an opening at my office for a receptionist—"

"I'm a science journalist, not a receptionist," Maya snapped, her frustration spilling over.

"And that's exactly the problem!" Sonia's patience frayed, her voice sharp. "Who cares about science in this country? No one's going to hire you for that."

"I care," Maya shot back, her tone defiant. "I care about the work I do."

"And where has that gotten you?" Sonia countered, shaking her head. "You're broke, Maya. You're broke, and the world isn't handing you jobs. Be practical."

Maya's jaw tightened, but she didn't respond. Instead, she stared into her coffee, its swirling surface a mirror of the storm inside her. From the corner of her eye, she noticed an older man at a nearby table. His gaze wasn't just lingering—it was fixed, cold and deliberate. Her stomach turned as she realized it wasn't her face he was looking at, but her breasts. She shifted uncomfortably, the heat of his scrutiny making her skin crawl.

She turned away sharply, disgusted, but the sensation lingered like an oily residue, a grim reminder of how the world seemed to strip her of her worth, reducing her existence to a shell of utility or desire.

Sonia pressed on, her tone softening. "I'll lend you the money again, but only if you take the job. You can't keep floating like this."

With that, Sonia stood, leaving a crumpled twenty-rupee note on the table to settle the coffee bill. "Think about it," she said firmly before walking out, leaving Maya alone with her thoughts.

The café buzzed faintly, but Maya barely noticed. Her eyes drifted to the empty chair across from her, then to the couple still lost in their private world. The old man's gaze had moved on, but its shadow clung to her mind, a quiet, gnawing reminder of her place in a universe that whispered only indifference.

Sonia wasn't wrong. Maya had once been a respected science journalist, a name that carried weight in academic and media circles alike. But her fall from grace was as swift as it was merciless, and the memories of it still burned vividly in her mind.

It had all started with an assignment from *Mumbai Slate*. They'd sent her to interview Dr. Harsh Nandan, the Science and Technology Minister. The piece was supposed to be a harmless puff article, complete with pre-approved questions crafted to paint the government in glowing hues. But such assignments grated at Maya. The scripted dishonesty, the thinly veiled propaganda—it all clashed with the ideals she once held sacred.

When the Minister began talking about incorporating Sanskrit into IIT curricula, she'd struggled to keep her disbelief hidden.

"Sanskrit? At science institutes?" she had asked cautiously, her voice carefully measured to mask her skepticism.

"Yes," Harsh had replied, his tone laced with the self-assuredness of someone unshaken by contradiction. "Our ancient scriptures hold the roots of modern science."

Maya's instincts as a journalist had flared like a warning beacon. "But don't you think we should prioritize contemporary research?" she had pressed, her attempt at diplomacy barely veiling her concern.

The Minister's expression had shifted, his demeanor hardening. "I'm done here," he had said curtly, yanking off his microphone before storming out of the interview.

That single, defiant question had unraveled her career. Within weeks, her assignments evaporated, editors stopped returning her calls, and her name became a whispered cautionary tale. The weight of irrelevance crushed her, an unspoken verdict from a world that rewarded conformity over integrity.

Perhaps, she had always been alone.

Maya had grown up in the shadows of neglect, shaped by absence and loss. Her father, a college watchman, worked long nights, leaving her to navigate childhood with only silence as a companion. Her mother had died before Maya could form a single memory of her—just a grainy wedding photograph remained, the only proof that she had once existed. A woman frozen in time, smiling at a future she never got to see.

Her best friend, Geeta, had been her only anchor, a rare burst of warmth in an otherwise muted world. Then, in the eighth standard, a single bad meal had taken Geeta away. Food poisoning, they had said. An accident. But Maya knew better—death was never just an accident. It was a thief, a relentless force that took and took until there was nothing left.

After that, she stopped trying. Good looks, intelligence—none of it mattered. She built walls instead, turned away from affection, rejected advances before they could become attachments. It was easier to be distant than to risk losing again.

And when her father's liver failed, when she sat beside his hospital bed and watched him slip away, she realized she had no one left. No family. No safety net. Just herself and the quiet, gnawing certainty that she belonged to no one and nowhere.

Death was an unstoppable force. It came for everyone, sooner or later. You never knew how far it was, nor the speed at which it approached. Sometimes, it blared its arrival with a slow, agonizing wail. Other times, it arrived without warning, standing beside you before you even knew it was near.

You could fear it, resist it, run from it—but in the end, it was the only certainty. Or you could accept it, embrace it like a lover, the only one truly loyal. It would hold your hand, whisper in the dark, and lead you away—not to salvation, not to damnation, but into the unknown, where suffering ceased and silence reigned.

Her phone buzzed, jolting her back to the present. She glanced at the screen: Nikhil Gaikwad. The name brought a wave of mixed emotions—it had been months since they'd last spoken.

"Hello?" she answered, her voice steadied by habit but hollow beneath the surface.

"*Maya! Long time. How've you been?*" Nikhil's voice carried an easy warmth, like an echo of a simpler time.

"I'm fine," she lied, the word tasting bitter in her mouth.

"*I've got something you might be interested in,*" he said, his tone laced with intrigue.

Her pulse quickened. "What kind of thing?"

A brief pause. "*Huh? Work.*"

She frowned. "What kind of work?"

His voice dropped slightly. *"Do you remember Vikram Jadhav?"*

"Of course. The botanist behind *Exotic World of Plants*. I interviewed him last year."

"Mumbai Slate wants another interview with him," Nikhil explained. *"And I thought you'd be perfect for it."*

Her breath caught. "Mumbai Slate? They won't work with me. Not after—"

"They know you're the best for this," Nikhil interrupted. *"Vikram isn't an easy man to interview. They need someone capable enough to handle him."*

"Then why didn't they call me directly?" she asked, suspicion creeping into her voice.

"You know why," he said gently. *"But they're willing to do this quietly. The contract will be in my name. You'll get paid, Maya."*

She hesitated, her pride warring with practicality. "But Vikram's been missing for almost a year. How am I supposed to find him?"

"That's the catch," Nikhil said. *"Nothing is easy. You'll have all expenses covered. Fifty thousand in advance."*

Maya exhaled slowly, the weight of her situation pressing against her resolve. The thought of someone else taking credit for her work stung, but the money—she needed the money. "Alright," she said finally, her voice tinged with reluctant acceptance.

"Great! You won't regret this," Nikhil said, satisfaction creeping into his tone. Then, after a brief pause, he added casually, *"And hey, once the job's done, let me take you out for lunch. Consider it a thank-you."*

She let out a small, tired laugh. "We'll see," she said, neither agreeing nor refusing. She had no other choice, and they both knew it.

After hanging up, she pulled out her phone and searched for Vikram Jadhav on LinkedIn. The profile appeared in the results, but it hadn't been updated in over a year. His last listed role was as a botany lecturer at Mumbai University. Maya frowned. It wasn't much to go on, but it was a start.

Stepping out of the café, Maya hailed a rickshaw. The air outside was thick with the noise and chaos of the city, a stark contrast to the quiet despair that lingered within her. As the rickshaw rattled down the crowded street, her fingers brushed against her old journalist badge tucked inside her bag. For the first time in months, she felt a faint flicker of hope—a fragile, wavering light in a universe that seemed perpetually indifferent.

Khandav

"Day 5, 5:00 pm -We are about to leave this forest, and that concludes our trip," Vikram's voice echoed into his recorder. The dense jungle swallowed the sound almost immediately, the thick air muffling even his deep baritone. He clicked the recorder off and stood still for a moment, the fading golden light casting a surreal glow over the towering trees. As the shadows stretched and intertwined, the vibrant forest transformed into something darker, heavier.

"We need to leave before the sun goes down," Vikram said, his tone calm but carrying an unmistakable edge of urgency. At fifty-five, Vikram's imposing frame and weathered appearance commanded respect. His broad shoulders carried the weight of decades spent exploring untamed landscapes, his khaki shirt stretched taut across his chest. Deep lines etched his face, a map of time and experience, framed by a salt-and-pepper beard that gave him an air of quiet authority. His piercing eyes missed little, scanning the jungle with a sharpness honed through years of fieldwork. A well-worn utility belt hung at his side, holding tools, a flashlight, and a sturdy knife—practical items that spoke to his preparedness for the unpredictable.

The group of seven post-grad students, however, remained oblivious to the subtle shift. Pooja, with her trusty DSLR slung around her neck, wandered away, snapping the last rays of sunlight filtering through the canopy. Nasreen, ever playful, plucked a vibrant flower and tucked it behind her ear, striking exaggerated poses for Pooja's lens. She pouted dramatically, arching her back with an air of mock seduction, drawing hearty laughter from the boys.

Vikram observed them, a faint smile tugging at his lips. Despite his stern demeanor, he had a soft spot for his students. Their energy reminded him of his younger self, though he often wondered if they understood the gravity of the world they sought to study. "You know, Darwin believed that trees have their heads in their roots," he said, his voice laced with both playfulness and authority, hoping to reel their attention back.

As expected, the group turned to him, curiosity piqued.

Praveen, the class clown, was quick to respond. "Which means," he said, gesturing upward, "they've got their asses waving in the air!"

Laughter rippled through the group. Even Vikram couldn't resist a small chuckle. "Exactly," he said, shaking his head at the crude humor. He pointed to the flower Nasreen had plucked. "And these," he added, "are the sex organs of trees. That's why they're so attractive."

Nasreen twirled the flower between her fingers, her grin mischievous. "Dick," she declared with mock dramatics, raising the flower to her nose for effect.

Vikram's smile lingered, but his thoughts drifted. Times had changed. Girls like Nasreen were bold, unfiltered in ways unimaginable during his youth. Yet, standing amidst this ancient jungle, he wondered how much of the natural world had truly evolved. Nature, after all, seemed timeless, unyielding to societal shifts.

Sanjay, deep in thought, suddenly spoke. "So… animals live straight up, and plants live upside down?" He blinked, processing his own words. "Wow, which means we live on others' waste?"

Praveen cackled. "A shit-eating cycle!"

Pooja wrinkled her nose. "Well, fruits aren't exactly plant shit."

Sanjay smirked. "Maybe not, but they're definitely made to be eaten so their seeds can spread."

That was when Vikram's gaze shifted—a mushroom, pale and damp, pushing through the rich soil. Something about it unsettled him. It stood apart from the cycle, thriving on decay, feeding on the dead. A silent recycler of the jungle's secrets.

Slowly, Vikram crouched, placing his recorder beside him. "But there's something far greater living beneath this forest," he said, his voice dropping into a more serious register. "Neither plant nor animal."

The students leaned in, sensing the shift in his demeanor.

"Fungus," he continued. He pointed to the mushroom. "And this… this is just its fruiting body."

Praveen snorted. "Looks like it too," he quipped, earning scattered chuckles.

Vikram ignored him. Carefully, he dug around the mushroom's base, revealing a network of white, slimy threads beneath. "This," he said, gesturing to the delicate web, "is part of a vast underground network. It connects the roots of every tree here. Nutrients, water, carbon—even information—travel through it. We call it the 'Wood Wide Web.'"

Nasreen's earlier playfulness was replaced by curiosity. "Like… an organic internet?" she asked, her brow furrowing.

Vikram nodded. Before he could elaborate, Sanjay, the quiet intellectual of the group, spoke up. "Maybe it's more like a collective brain. A jungle brain."

Nasreen shot him a skeptical glance. "A brain? You think the jungle thinks?"

Sanjay pushed his glasses up, his expression serene. "Why not?" he replied. "Maybe it thinks slowly. Trees live on a timeline so different from ours that their thoughts would seem incomprehensible."

"Like a dog versus a fly?" Praveen asked, scratching his head. "A fly's brain works faster. Does that mean it's smarter?"

"Of course not," Nasreen interjected. "Dogs are way smarter. They have more complex network of neurons."

Sanjay smiled faintly. "Maybe. But speed doesn't always equal intelligence. A slow-thinking entity might understand the world in ways we can't."

Vikram watched the exchange, his smile returning. This was what he loved—minds expanding, grappling with the mysteries of nature. "So," Praveen asked, placing his hands on the ground, "what do you think these trees are thinking right now?"

"They probably hate us," Nandu, the group's lovable joker, replied, his grin wide. Another wave of laughter broke out, but it was shorter this time. The jungle had grown unnervingly quiet. The once lively chorus of birds and insects had dimmed, leaving only the faint rustling of leaves as the wind picked up.

Pooja raised her camera again, hesitating before taking another shot. Even she seemed to sense the shift. Nasreen plucked the flower from her ear, studying it as her earlier lightheartedness ebbed away. "Plant dick! This feels… wrong," she murmured, dropping the flower to the ground.

Vikram stood, brushing dirt from his hands. "Enough theories," he said, his tone firm. "The sun's setting, and this jungle becomes dangerous at night. We need to leave. Now."

The students hurried to gather their belongings, their earlier camaraderie fading as the encroaching darkness pressed in. Vikram's gaze drifted back to the mushroom. Its pale cap was now half-shrouded in shadow, the encroaching night transforming it into something ominous. The jungle itself seemed alive, its long shadows twisting and reaching as if to envelop them.

"Watch your step," Vikram warned, his voice sharp. "These woods are famous for their poisonous snakes."

The group fell silent, his words sinking in. What had been a place of wonder and discovery now felt foreboding—a living entity, watching and waiting as daylight faded.

The yellow minibus idled on the narrow tar road, its engine grumbling softly as the jungle around it seemed to hold its breath. The last rays of sunlight slanted through the canopy, casting long, twisted shadows across the muddy path that branched off into the dense underbrush. The air grew colder, heavier, as though the forest itself was preparing for something.

The driver revved the engine, jolting the bus forward.

"Damn! Stop!" Vikram's voice rang out sharply, cutting through the encroaching silence. He leaned toward the driver, irritation etched on his weathered face. "Five minutes—my recorder! Shit! Wait here for five or ten minutes."

The bus groaned to a halt. Inside, the students stirred, their chatter fading as they peered out of the windows. Vikram turned to them, his imposing figure framed by the fading daylight. At fifty-five, his broad shoulders and salt-and-pepper beard gave him the air of a man who had weathered countless challenges. Yet, as he looked toward the jungle, even he felt a subtle unease creeping into his thoughts. The forest seemed darker than it should have been, its shadows unnaturally dense.

"Forgot my notes," he said tersely, already stepping off the bus. "Sit tight, I'll be back in ten minutes."

As Vikram began striding toward the jungle, the faint hum of an approaching motor broke the stillness. A wobbly moped appeared, carrying a short, stocky man who seemed ill-suited to the growing darkness. His crisp white shirt clung to his damp skin, and his khaki pants, tucked into scuffed police boots, gave him an air of misplaced authority. His chest puffed out as he parked the moped and dismounted, but his darting eyes betrayed his unease.

The man skidded to a halt, quickly dismounting. "Where are you going?" he called out, his voice tight with urgency.

Vikram paused, turning to face him. "Into the jungle," he replied simply, resuming his pace.

"You can't go," the man said, stepping in front of him, his breath coming in short bursts.

The students inside the bus exchanged uneasy glances. Some began to climb out, curiosity mingling with apprehension as they watched the confrontation.

"And who are you to tell me that?" Vikram demanded, annoyance flickering in his sharp gaze.

The man straightened his back, though his voice wavered. "I am Baburao Kamble, forest officer of this region," he declared. In truth, Baburao was a low-ranking forest worker, tasked with patrolling the edges of the jungle. But he clung to his title as if it were a shield.

Vikram's expression hardened. "Listen," he said firmly, "I'm a professor at a government college. This trip is government-sponsored. We've toured the entire Konkan region, and this was our last stop. Now, we're heading back to Mumbai. I just forgot my voice recorder in the jungle—all my notes are on it."

Baburao's face darkened. He gestured for Vikram to step aside, away from the students. Lowering his voice to a near whisper, he said, "Forget about your notes. The sun is going down."

Vikram frowned, glancing at the treeline where the shadows were deepening into an almost solid wall of darkness. "It'll take ten minutes. I can see the spot from here."

Baburao's eyes flicked nervously toward the jungle. He leaned in closer, his voice trembling. "You don't understand. Can't you smell the hunger? Their eagerness? The wind is blowing toward us." And tonight…" He paused, his breath hitching. "Tonight is the full moon."

Vikram raised an eyebrow, unimpressed. "So?"

Baburao's face remained grave. His eyes darted to the students, then back to Vikram. "This jungle… it's not like others. On full moon nights, it comes alive. People hear voices, see things that don't belong to this world. It calls to them."

Overhearing the exchange, the students' smirks faded. Even Vikram couldn't suppress the faintest hint of unease. The forest seemed darker now, its silence unnatural, oppressive.

"So, the jungle kept my recorder on purpose?" Vikram asked dryly, though his voice lacked its usual confidence. "It's trying to lure me in?"

Baburao's face didn't change. "I'm warning you," he said, louder now, his voice tinged with desperation. "If you go back in there, you might not come out. You need to leave. Now."

Vikram hesitated, glancing at the students who were now uncharacteristically quiet. The shadows from the forest seemed to reach toward him, as if urging him to stay put.

But fear was not an option. He couldn't waver—not to superstition, not to whispers in the dark, and certainly not in front of his students. He turned to Salim, the driver, who was leaning against the bus, his arms crossed. "Salim, keep an eye on them," Vikram said, his tone clipped but steady. "I'll be back in fifteen minutes—no more." His voice carried confidence, but deep inside, the oppressive weight of the jungle was beginning to claw at his resolve."

Baburao stepped back, his face a mixture of resignation and fear. "Are your notes worth your life?" he asked quietly.

But Vikram shrugged off the warning. "Ghosts don't belong in science," he said, striding toward the jungle with calm determination.

Baburao sighed heavily, defeated. "Fine. Then I'll come with you," he muttered, following reluctantly.

"Kids!" Vikram's voice called back sharply. "Don't roam around. Sit in the bus. Salim, keep an eye on things."

The students watched the two men disappear into the thickening shadows. The jungle seemed to swallow them whole, its trees leaning in like silent sentinels.

The jungle closed in quickly. As the two men walked deeper, the air grew colder, the silence heavy. Though Vikram's skepticism remained, Baburao's fear was palpable. Every step he took seemed to weigh heavier, as if the jungle itself resisted their presence.

"Have you ever actually seen any ghosts?" Vikram asked casually, though his voice carried an edge of tension.

Baburao glanced around nervously. "No," he admitted. "Not in fifteen years. But the villagers… they've seen things. Just last month, Parvati—one of the women from the village—went into the jungle to collect wood. She saw her husband standing among the trees, calling to her."

Vikram raised an eyebrow. "And what's strange about that?"

Baburao's voice dropped to a whisper. "Her husband has been dead for three years."

Vikram said nothing, but the chill that crept up his spine was hard to ignore. The shadows around them seemed to stretch and twist, the trees whispering secrets only they could hear.

"There!" Vikram said suddenly, spotting his recorder lying beside a pale mushroom. He stepped forward, relief washing over him.

Baburao, however, remained rooted in place, his eyes darting around as if the jungle itself might pounce.

Vikram picked up the recorder, clicking it on. His voice felt oddly out of place in the thickening gloom. "Day 5: evening, 5:45. Got my recorder back. Time to..." His words trailed off, swallowed by the oppressive silence that had settled over the jungle like a blanket of dread.

A strange sensation washed over him—a prickling at the back of his neck, as if unseen eyes were watching him from the shadows. His heart skipped a beat. He glanced around, trying to shake the feeling. The trees, their branches twisted and gnarled, seemed to lean closer, as if they were listening. It was like that eerie feeling when you're convinced someone—or something— is watching you, someone long gone. It's the sensation you get entering your dead father's old room or sitting near your late dog's empty doghouse. Maybe the location ignites buried memories. But this wasn't a place of memories. This wasn't his father's room or any familiar haunt. This was an alien forest, an unknown wilderness—one that held nothing of his past, yet still felt disturbingly alive.

"What happened?" Baburao's voice broke the silence, but it sounded distant, muffled by the thick air. He was looking at Vikram with concern.

"Nothing..." Vikram replied, though his voice was uncertain. His gaze drifted to the narrow path between the trees. The shadows there were deeper, almost unnatural, as if the darkness itself was alive, breathing. Was someone standing there? A figure, barely discernible, seemed to shift in the murk.

"Who's there?" Vikram's voice was louder now, edged with both curiosity and a creeping sense of unease.

Baburao squinted, confused. "There's no one," he said, but his voice wavered. He took a step back, instinctively inching closer to Vikram.

Then, the voice came.

"Vikky..."

The word was soft at first, almost a whisper carried by the wind, but it echoed through the trees, weaving its way through the branches, growing louder. It was a voice Vikram hadn't heard in nearly twenty years, yet it was unmistakable—haunting, familiar, and deeply wrong. His breath caught in his throat as he turned, searching the shadows.

"Vikky... Brother..."

Vikram froze, his mind struggling to process the impossible. His pulse quickened, pounding in his ears. The shadows parted just enough for him to see—a boy, no more than eighteen, his figure flickering in and out of view like a mirage. He stood between the trees, barely lit by the dying light, his face pale and gaunt. It was Shyam, Vikram's younger brother—his brother who had been dead for more than twenty years.

"I am so lonely, Vikky..." the boy's voice whispered again, reverberating through the trees, making the air feel thick and suffocating.

Vikram's legs felt like lead. He stood dumbfounded, torn between disbelief and the overwhelming urge to run to the boy.

Part of him wanted to embrace his brother, to feel the warmth of his presence once more. But the rational side of his mind fought back. It wasn't real—it couldn't be. His scientific mind screamed in denial, yet the sight of Shyam's sorrowful eyes cut through him like a knife.

"Shyamu?" Vikram's voice cracked. His body moved forward instinctively, but a firm hand grabbed him from behind.

"Damn!" Baburao hissed, his voice barely a whisper. His fingers dug into Vikram's arm as he held him back, his eyes wide with terror. "Sir! Get a hold of yourself!"

But Vikram didn't hear him. His gaze was locked on the boy in the shadows, his heart breaking all over again. "Brother..." he whispered, tears welling up in his eyes. "Shyamu!"

"Vikky, don't leave me," the ghostly figure called out, its voice laced with despair. "I'm so lonely..."

Vikram's heart twisted, his rationality crumbling beneath the weight of his grief. He took another step toward the trees, reaching out as if he could pull his brother from the darkness. His hand trembled.

"Sir! There's no one there!" Baburao's voice was frantic now, desperate. He slapped Vikram hard across the face, jolting him. "It's a ghost! Run!"

But Vikram was in a trance, his body torn between reality and the past, his mind slipping into the memories of a life long gone. His brother was there—he could see him, hear him. His brother was reaching out to him. He couldn't leave him. Not again.

"Shyamu..." Vikram's voice broke into a sob. He struggled against Baburao's grip, pulling free and stumbling toward the figure. Tears streamed down his face as he reached out, desperate to hold his brother one more time.

But as he neared the figure, the shadows seemed to shift unnaturally, the edges of Shyamu's form flickering like a broken projection. His face twisted, elongating unnaturally. His eyes, once sad, now glowed faintly, like embers in the dark. His mouth stretched into a wide, eerie grin that didn't belong on a human face.

"Brother..." Shyam's voice, once soft and pleading, turned mocking, hollow. "Don't leave me, Vikky... Don't leave me here..."

Vikram's breath caught in his throat as he froze, realizing with sickening clarity that whatever this was—it wasn't his brother.

Baburao's voice snapped him back. "Run! We have to run!" He yanked Vikram back, pulling him with all his strength. But Vikram's legs wouldn't move. He stumbled, falling to his knees as he looked back at the thing that wore his brother's face.

"Shyamu..." Vikram sobbed, his heart breaking all over again.

But the figure didn't move toward him. It only stood there, its eyes glowing brighter, its grin widening unnaturally. "Don't go, Vikky... I'm so lonely here... I'm waiting for you..."

Vikram's mind spun, caught between grief and horror. He struggled to his feet, but his legs felt like they were sinking into the earth. Baburao slapped him again, harder this time, dragging him back, his own breath coming in ragged gasps.

"Sir, it's not real! It's the jungle—it's the damn jungle playing tricks!" Baburao yelled, pulling Vikram further back. His voice was barely holding together, his own fear bubbling to the surface.

The recorder had fallen to the ground, its red light blinking in the dark, unnoticed. Baburao snatched it up, not daring to look back at the figure in the trees. He kept pulling Vikram, his voice tight with urgency. "We have to go. Do you hear me? We have to go!"

Vikram gave one last look into the trees, his heart shattering as he saw Shyam standing there, his figure now barely more than a shadow. The boy's face was twisted with sadness, his eyes glowing faintly in the darkness. "Don't leave me, Vikky... Don't leave me brother..."

Baburao didn't wait any longer. He pulled Vikram with all his might, and they stumbled away from the clearing, the oppressive air closing in behind them. Vikram turned, his face wet with tears, his body shaking as they fled back into the jungle.

Behind them, the eerie voice echoed one last time, haunting the trees. "I'm so lonely... Vicky"

Praveen, restless and bored, picked up a stone and hurled it toward the thick jungle. It vanished into the shadows without a sound, swallowed whole by the darkening trees. "It's already been more than 20 minutes!" he groaned, frustration creeping into his voice. "Nothing's more boring than waiting around."

"Okay, let's do something," Nandu chimed in, eager to break the monotony.

"Like what?" Nasreen asked, folding her arms, already feeling the unease of the jungle creeping into her bones.

Praveen's eyes lit up with a mischievous glint. "Let's name this place!" he suggested, his grin wide.

The others exchanged curious glances, intrigued by the idea. "Good idea," Pooja agreed, snapping a picture of the group. "Who knows, maybe the name will stick!"

The kids looked around, sizing up the eerie landscape around them, the trees now mere silhouettes against the fading light. The once vibrant green foliage was now cloaked in shadow, every branch and leaf seeming to twist and writhe as the jungle breathed around them.

Praveen, excited, turned to the driver. "Can you bring the name slate from our camp?"

The driver, seemingly unfazed by the rising tension, shuffled to the bus and returned with an old wooden stand and a nameplate reading "Tiger Camp." Praveen and Nandu dug a small hole at the junction where the muddy path veered off from the tar road and led deeper into the jungle's mouth. They placed the board so it pointed ominously down the dark path.

"How's that?" Praveen exclaimed, stepping back to admire their work.

Pooja gave a thumbs-up, but Nasreen frowned. "Tiger Camp? That doesn't sound right for a place like this," she muttered, shaking her head.

Nandu laughed, the sound oddly hollow in the growing darkness. "How about Ghost Jungle?" he suggested, only half-joking.

Sanjay, who had been quiet until now, spoke up with a solemn edge to his voice. "Khandav. Name it Khandav."

Everyone turned to him, their curiosity piqued. "Khandav?" Nasreen repeated, the name rolling off her tongue like a whispered warning.

Sanjay's gaze was distant, as if he were lost in thought. "In the Mahabharata, the Pandavas burned down Khandav Jungle to satisfy the god Agni," he explained, his voice low and almost reverent. "All the plants, animals, and insects—everything was reduced to ash. Krishna and Arjun didn't let a single creature escape. They slaughtered anything that tried to run. And after, they built their grand city, Indraprastha, on the remains. Khandav is the first recorded example of humanity's destruction of nature, of perversion in the name of progress."

The group fell silent, the weight of his words settling over them like a dark cloud. The jungle seemed to respond, its shadows deepening, the air growing heavier.

"Gimme the paint," Nandu finally said, his voice subdued. He dipped the brush into the thick, black paint and began painting over the nameplate. "Khandav," he murmured as he scrawled the letters, each stroke deliberate. When he was done, the word dripped down the wooden board like blood, the wet paint forming jagged, horror-like shapes.

Praveen nodded, approving. "Khandav. That sounds right."

Both Nasreen and Pooja gave him a thumbs-up, though their smiles were laced with uncertainty.

Just as they finished, the rustling of leaves drew their attention. Baburao stumbled out of the jungle, his face pale and drenched in sweat. He was holding onto Vikram, who was trembling, tears streaking his face. Baburao's breaths came in heavy, ragged gasps as if the very air had been sucked from his lungs.

The kids rushed toward them. Praveen and Nandu reached Vikram first, their faces creased with concern. "What happened?" Praveen asked, his voice shaking.

Baburao bent over, hands on his knees, still gasping for breath. His eyes were wide, filled with a primal fear that the students hadn't seen before. "Ghost…" he wheezed, each word a struggle. "Jungle…"

The students exchanged nervous glances. The humor and lightheartedness that had filled the air earlier was gone, replaced by something cold, something that crawled under their skin.

"Get in the bus!" Baburao finally managed to shout, his voice laced with desperation. "Run! Get out—quick!"

Vikram stumbled forward, his movements shaky, his mind still trapped in the nightmare of what he'd just seen. The driver, sensing the urgency, had already started the engine, his own hands trembling slightly as he gripped the wheel.

Confused, the students hesitated. But then Baburao shouted again, louder this time, his voice filled with a terror that made the hair on their arms stand on end. "Run!"

The kids didn't wait for a third command. They scrambled into the bus, their previous bravado gone, replaced by silent fear. The driver revved the engine, his foot already on the accelerator, as the last of them climbed inside.

As the bus jerked into motion, Baburao came running after them, shouting, "Stop! Wait!"

The bus screeched to a halt. Baburao reached them, his hand shaking as he thrust Vikram's voice recorder into Praveen's hands. "Here," he said, still panting heavily.

The kids stared at him, confused and scared. The bus driver wasted no time. As soon as Baburao backed away, the engine roared, and the bus sped off, the students too shaken to speak.

Baburao stood there, watching them disappear down the road. His breath was still uneven, his body trembling. He turned slowly toward the jungle, where the trees now loomed darker, more menacing than before. His gaze fell on the nameplate they had just painted. "Khandav." The fresh paint was already starting to drip, forming eerie, jagged shapes that resembled twisted letters, like something cursed.

For a moment, Baburao considered removing the sign, wiping away the name, but his hand froze in mid-air. His instincts told him something—something that made the skin on the back of his neck prickle. It was too late now.

The box of paint lay at his feet. He crouched down, his fingers trembling as he picked up the brush. Without thinking, he dipped it into the black paint and slowly drew a thick, black cross over the name. A warning. A curse. A sign that no one should ever go there again.

He wiped his forehead with his sleeve, mounted his moped, and kicked it into gear. His eyes flickered once more toward the jungle before he sped off into the darkening twilight, the thick trees seeming to close in behind him.

Behind him, the jungle remained still, but the name on the sign bled in the darkness. "Khandav." A place now marked by something ancient, something malevolent. Something that was waiting.

From deep within the jungle, a faint sound emerged. It wasn't the wind. It wasn't an animal. It was something else—a low, guttural whisper that rose and fell, carrying an unspoken promise of dread. Baburao didn't look back.

The Damsel in Distress

"This is the way the world ends, not with a bang but a whimper."

– T.S. Eliot, *The Hollow Men*

Swati Seth had to be at the party by 8:00 sharp. In her early thirties, Swati carried herself with the confidence of someone accustomed to turning heads. Her fair skin, sharp features, and perfectly styled long hair made her impossible to ignore, while the elegant fragrance of her perfume lingered subtly in her wake. The golden dress she wore hugged her figure, shimmering with every movement. It revealed just enough to captivate but never too much to appear gauche. Swati wasn't a household name—just a small-time model with influence in niche circles—but she treated every event like a stepping stone to something greater.

The red Verna glided smoothly along the dimly lit highway as she pressed the accelerator, making up for lost time. The glow of her golden dress shimmered faintly in the dashboard's light, a quiet reflection of her determination.

Her phone buzzed, interrupting the rhythm of the music streaming through the speakers. The sound dipped as the Bluetooth took over. Swati tapped the screen to answer.

"Hello, Swati!" A familiar male voice filled the cabin.

"Hey, Prakash! Where are you?" Her voice was bright, her energy infectious.

"Just got back from Goa," Prakash replied, the hum of road noise audible on his end.

"Oh, nice! Coming to the party tonight or not?" she teased.

"That's why I called. You'll be there, right?" His voice carried a hint of excitement that pleased her.

"Of course, I'm going! We've got a lot to talk about, darling."

"What's the plan after the party?" Prakash asked, his tone playful, carrying a mischievous edge.

Swati chuckled. "Ah, men are dogs…" she said, drawing out the joke, her laughter light. "Maybe we'll stay together. Who knows?"

Prakash laughed along, but before she could respond, a strange, rhythmic thumping sound began to emerge from beneath the car. The steering wheel shuddered slightly in her hands. The unsettling noise grew louder, interrupting the conversation.

"Damn," she muttered, pulling the car over to the side of the road. The Verna rolled to a stop beneath a flickering streetlight, the oppressive darkness pressing in on all sides.

"What happened?" Prakash asked, his voice faint through the speakers.

"Flat tire," Swati replied, stepping out of the car. The night air hit her bare shoulders, the faint breeze tugging at her dress. Her heels clicked against the asphalt as she inspected the damage. The driver's-side tire was completely deflated, sagging lifelessly against the rim.

"Do you have a spare?" Prakash's voice sounded distant now, as if the night itself was swallowing the sound.

"Yeah, I do," she replied, brushing her hair away from her face. The chill of the night prickled her skin. "See you at the party, honey. I'll handle this."

"Alright. Call me if you run into trouble. See you, love."

"See you," Swati replied, slipping the phone into her clutch.

The road around her was eerily quiet. The occasional rustle of leaves and the distant chirp of crickets were the only sounds. Faint headlights appeared far in the distance, only to vanish moments later, leaving her enveloped once again in the heavy, oppressive dark.

Leaning against the car, she let her eyes scan the stretch of road, up and down. The isolation was unnerving. The breeze whispered through the surrounding trees, carrying a hollow, unnatural sound that made her skin crawl. She sighed, taking a deep breath before opening the trunk.

She stared at the spare tire for a moment, her lips pressing into a thin line. Though a model, Swati prided herself on her fitness and independence. Physical tasks didn't intimidate her. But the thought of messing up her beautiful dress gnawed at her. Hours of preparation felt at risk of being undone by the dirt and grime of roadside repairs.

With a resigned sigh, she bent forward to lift the jack and spare tire. The golden fabric clung to her figure as she moved, a striking contrast to the cold, grimy tools in the trunk.

Manoj Sharma zigzagged the bike down the dark highway, a cigarette clamped between his lips. Kamlesh Tripathi, drunk and giggling like a fool, clung to him loosely, swaying on the seat. Behind them, Dilip Kokate grumbled, trying to hold on without falling off.

"Oi, ride straight, idiot! You'll get us killed," Dilip growled, bracing himself.

"Relax, yaar! This bike rides smooth as butter. We'll make some solid cash off it," Manoj said, exhaling smoke into the cool night air.

"Where'd you pick this beauty from?" Dilip asked, grinning as the breeze hit his face.

"That dumbass Pandu—the shop guy from the corner where we buy smokes," Kamlesh giggled, slurring his words.

"Arre, that idiot?" Manoj chuckled.

"Yeah, bro! The moron went inside with his bags and just left the bike there—keys still in the ignition!" Kamlesh howled.

"Motherfucker is gonna cry," Dilip snorted, shaking his head.

Their laughter slowed as the bike approached the roadside, where something caught their eye—a woman in a shimmering golden dress, bent over the open trunk of a red Verna. She was struggling with a spare tire, her figure arching just enough to make their mouths water.

"Check that out, boys," Manoj muttered, his cigarette dangling between his fingers.

"Hot stuff," Dilip whispered, his gaze fixed on her legs glistening under the flickering streetlight. Her heels wobbled as she struggled, the movement making her seem both vulnerable and alluring.

"Madam needs some help," Manoj grinned slyly. "Let's be good boys, shall we?"

The three exchanged wicked glances. Manoj eased the bike to a stop behind the car, far enough to avoid detection.

"Kamlesh, stay on the bike. You'll mess things up if you open your mouth," Manoj said, tossing him a warning look.

Kamlesh giggled. "No worries, boss! I'm here to enjoy the view."

Manoj and Dilip approached the car casually. Swati was still wrestling with the tire when they reached her.

"Need a hand, miss?" Manoj asked, his grin too smooth to be sincere.

Swati turned, startled but relieved. "Ah... Yeah, that'd be great. This thing's heavier than it looks."

"No worries. We're mechanics—just test-riding that bike after a repair," Manoj lied smoothly.

She hesitated but nodded. "How much?"

"Whatever you think is fair. We'll swap the tire, but you'll need to get the puncture fixed down the road," Manoj said.

"Okay, thanks." Swati stepped aside, glancing nervously at her phone.

Dilip grabbed the jack and the spare tire, loosening the bolts with practiced ease. Manoj kept close to Swati, striking up small talk to distract her.

"Not from around here, are you?" Manoj asked casually.

"Just passing through, on my way to the city," Swati replied, folding her arms as unease flickered across her face.

"The city's still about an hour away. You should get the tire fixed soon—don't wanna get stuck out here at night," Manoj said, inching closer.

"Yeah, I will," she said, stepping slightly away and pulling out her phone. "Excuse me, I need to make a quick call."

Swati moved a few steps away, dialing her mom. Her voice was calm but brisk. "Hey, Mom… Yeah, I'll be late. Tomorrow evening, okay?… Of course, I'll be there." She moved further from the car, her words fading into the night.

Manoj nudged Dilip, who gave a knowing grin. He tightened the last bolt and began packing the punctured tire into the trunk. As he reached for the lid, Manoj placed a hand on it, stopping him.

"Oi, wait a second. What's that?" Manoj asked, squinting into the trunk.

Swati, now off the phone, walked back over. "What?"

"Looks like an earring or something," Manoj said, pretending to peer into the shadows.

Swati leaned forward to look. "I don't see anything."

In one swift motion, Manoj shoved her forward, sending her sprawling into the trunk.

"Gotcha, sweetheart," he sneered as Swati let out a muffled scream.

Dilip climbed in after her, his knife glinting in the dim light. He pressed it to her throat, grinning sadistically. "Move, and I'll cut you," he hissed.

Manoj slammed the trunk shut, muffling her cries. Inside, the cramped space reeked of metal and fear. Dilip's breath was hot against Swati's skin as she whimpered.

"Relax, darling. We'll have a good time," Dilip whispered mockingly, running his fingers over her thigh.

The muffled sound of the car door opening echoed as Kamlesh climbed into the passenger seat, still giggling drunkenly. "Good catch, boys."

"Shut up and let's move," Manoj barked, turning the key in the ignition. The engine roared to life, headlights slicing through the night.

Swati's muffled cries filled the trunk as Dilip loomed over her, his shadowy form a sinister blur. The car sped down the empty road, leaving nothing behind but silence and the abandoned bike.

Manoj had been driving for a while, gripping the wheel with one hand while the other rested on the gearstick. The road was mostly empty, but the noises from the trunk were growing louder—thuds and muffled cries mixed with occasional banging.

In the cramped darkness of the trunk, Swati was paralyzed by fear. A knife pressed cold and unyielding against her neck, while a male hand roamed her body with cruel intent—squeezing, pinching, scratching at will. She wanted to fight, to claw her way out, but the blade grazing her skin held her still. Her mind raced, desperate to understand how she had ended up here.

What went wrong? Over and over, she traced the simple steps of her day, replaying them endlessly. If she had just taken a different route, if she had been quicker to notice the signs, if she had run when she had the chance… Every scenario unfolded in her mind, each ending the same way, with her trapped in this nightmare.

And then it happened. The hand slid beneath her waistband, rough fingers violating her last shred of dignity. Even with the knife pressed against her throat, the scream tore from her lips, raw and guttural. She couldn't contain it—her body, her soul, rebelled against the horror of it all.

"That motherfucker Dilip is already on her," Manoj muttered under his breath, irritation flickering across his face.

Kamlesh, slumped in the passenger seat, giggled. "What's your problem, bhai? You wanted first dibs?"

"There's no 'first' with her, idiot," Manoj snapped, his eyes scanning the road. "We all get our turn." His real problem wasn't jealousy—it was the noise. If anyone heard those sounds at the wrong moment, they were screwed.

The car approached a bend where a dimly lit shop stood—a small, shabby store with a peeling sign that read *Alankar Store*. Outside, the display was a clutter of general supplies and electrical items. Manoj slowed the car and brought it to a sharp stop.

"I need to shut this shit down," he grumbled, more to himself than to Kamlesh.

He climbed out, scanning the street quickly before walking into the store. The shopkeeper, a plump, middle-aged man dressed in wrinkled white pajamas and a loose shirt, looked up from behind the counter, struggling to rise from his wooden stool.

"Binding or packaging tapes?" Manoj asked curtly, his tone impatient.

The shopkeeper shuffled around, pulling open creaky drawers and placing four rolls of tape on the counter.

Manoj picked up two of them. "These are enough." His gaze drifted toward a coil of rope hanging on the wall. "That rope too. And that tennis ball," he added, pointing lazily.

"How many meters?" the shopkeeper asked, eyeing the rope.

Manoj stared at him, the muscles in his jaw tightening. "Three. That'll do."

The shopkeeper, moving at an agonizing pace, uncoiled the rope, measured three meters, and cut it with rusty scissors. His fingers were slow and clumsy, and every second made Manoj more anxious. The clock was ticking. The noises from the trunk needed to stop before they drew any unwanted attention.

"Here you go." The shopkeeper handed him the rope and tennis ball. "380 rupees. You headed to the city?" he asked, trying to make small talk.

Manoj slapped 400 rupees on the counter. "Keep the change."

Just as the shopkeeper reached for the cash, a loud bang echoed from the trunk of the Verna outside. The shopkeeper froze, his eyes narrowing with suspicion.

"What's in the trunk?" he asked, his hand hovering near the drawer filled with rolls of tape.

Manoj's eyes darkened, annoyance bubbling into something dangerous. He stepped closer, his voice low and deliberate. "You got something behind that door, huh?" he asked, nodding toward the storeroom door behind the counter.

The shopkeeper blinked, confused and uneasy.

"Or maybe something stashed in these drawers?" Manoj hissed, slapping the side of the counter, making the old man flinch.

The shopkeeper, caught between fear and confusion, stammered, "I—I just asked—"

"Saala, can't mind your own fucking business, can you?" Manoj snarled, closing the distance between them.

Before the shopkeeper could react, Manoj plunged a knife deep into the man's neck. The blade sliced through skin and muscle, cutting off the man's words with a wet, choking gurgle.

The shopkeeper staggered backward, clutching desperately at his throat, blood pouring through his fingers. As he collapsed to the floor, he pulled a few drawers down with him, their contents spilling across the ground. One hand clutched uselessly at the wound in his neck, while the other still gripped a roll of tape.

Manoj stood over him, watching with cold detachment as the man gasped and writhed, his life draining out onto the dirty floor.

"You wanted to know what's in the trunk?" Manoj muttered, wiping the blade on the man's shirt before slipping it back into his pocket. "You should've just stayed quiet." Manoj grabbed the bag with the tapes, rope, and tennis ball, giving one last look at the lifeless body sprawled on the floor.

Without another word, he walked back to the car, slamming the shop door shut behind him.

The jungle seemed untouched, ancient and indifferent, except for the lone road cutting through it. The red Verna, tearing through the stillness, was a scar on the silence.

The car's headlights split the thick fog, casting eerie shapes into the dark undergrowth, while the December moonlight bathed the landscape in a pale, ghostly blue.

Inside the car, the men settled into the drive. Dilip, bald and built like a wrestler, gripped the wheel, navigating with quiet focus. On the radio, a bollywood number blared: *"Bidi jalaile jigar se piya…"*

In the passenger seat, Manoj rolled down the window, taking in the cool air with a cigarette perched between his fingers. He inhaled deeply, savoring the smoke, and glanced back at Kamlesh, slumped on the back seat, reeking of cheap alcohol.

"I killed that motherfucker," Manoj said flatly, blowing a cloud of smoke out the window.

Kamlesh blinked, his mind slow to catch up. "What? Who?"

"The shopkeeper," Manoj replied, flicking ash carelessly.

Kamlesh sat up slightly, confused. "What the hell for? We only needed tape and rope."

Manoj chuckled darkly. "The bastard got too interested in our business. So, I ended his."

Kamlesh shifted uneasily. "You could've just left, man…"

"Yeah? And what if he talked?" Manoj asked, giving him a look.

Dilip let out a bark of laughter. "One less nosy bastard! That's a public service, if you ask me."

Manoj's eyes flicked to the small Ganesh idol on the dashboard, sneering. "Look at this. The bitch believes in God."

"So what?" Dilip said, his voice a little defensive. "I believe too."

"Yeah, I know. Didn't Kamlesh go to Shirdi last month?" Manoj grinned, twisting the knife just for fun.

Kamlesh shifted nervously in his seat. "Yeah... so?"

Manoj's grin widened. "I bet you prayed for a chick to fuck, didn't you?"

Kamlesh frowned. "Come on, man. Don't joke about that stuff."

Manoj laughed, enjoying their discomfort. "Maybe the bitch in the trunk prayed to get fucked by three guys. Gods work in mysterious ways, huh?"

Kamlesh muttered under his breath, annoyed but too scared to confront him. Dilip kept his focus on the road, his jaw tight. Manoj always pushed too far, and they knew better than to argue.

Then, the noise came.

Thud. Thud. Thud.

The sound echoed from the trunk—dull, deliberate, and insistent. Swati was fighting her bonds again.

All three men went silent for a moment, exchanging glances.

Manoj sighed, grinding his cigarette out on the dashboard. "This fucking bitch," he muttered.

"I like this song," Dilip said quietly, still trying to focus on the road.

"Then shove it up your ass," Manoj snapped. "And stop the fucking car."

Dilip reached forward, turning off the radio without a word, but kept driving.

"I said STOP THE FUCKING CAR!" Manoj roared, slamming a hand against the dashboard.

Dilip gritted his teeth, flicked the hazard lights on, and pulled over to the side of the empty road.

All three men got out, the jungle around them a black void, with only the faint rustling of leaves in the cool breeze.

Kamlesh stumbled to the trunk, fumbled with the key, and popped it open. Inside, Swati lay curled, her arms and legs bound with tape. A tennis ball was stuffed into her mouth, held in place by more tape wrapped around her face. Her wide, terrified eyes darted between the three men as she struggled and made desperate, muffled sounds.

"Shut the fuck up," Manoj hissed, slapping her hard across the face. Her head snapped to the side as she whimpered.

"Not a sound, understand?" Manoj snarled. He pulled out a revolver, pressing the cold barrel against her forehead. "Not one fucking sound."

Swati trembled, her breath hitching as she fought the urge to cry. Manoj leaned closer, wrapping a hand around her throat and squeezing just enough to make her gag.

"When I say stop the car, Dilip, you stop the fucking car." Manoj didn't take his eyes off Swati as he spoke, his hand tightening on her neck. She squirmed under his grip, her muffled cries growing fainter.

Dilip stared at Manoj, then lowered his eyes. "Alright, man. I got it," he muttered, defeated.

Just then, a yellow headlight appeared in the distance, growing brighter as it approached.

"Fuck!" Kamlesh cursed. The three men stood frozen as the light drew closer.

A man on a Vespa scooter appeared from around the bend, slowing down as he noticed the car pulled over. His eyes widened in shock when he saw Swati in the trunk, writhing and trying to scream through the gag.

The rider panicked, twisting the throttle and speeding away.

"Stop, you bastard!" Kamlesh shouted, running after the Vespa, his drunken steps uneven but fast.

Manoj slammed the trunk shut with a loud *thud* and jumped back into the car. "Go!" he barked at Dilip, who hit the gas.

The car roared down the road, headlights slicing through the fog as they chased the fleeing scooter. The man was so terrified, his hands shook uncontrollably. He lost control, skidding off the road and tumbling to the ground, his leg pinned under the fallen Vespa.

As he struggled to free himself, Kamlesh reached him first, pouncing like a predator.

The man managed to stand, limping and bleeding, but Kamlesh tackled him from behind, slamming him into the road with a laugh.

Manoj and Dilip pulled the car to a stop, watching from the headlights as Kamlesh dragged the man toward the trunk.

"Please! I didn't see anything! I swear I won't tell anyone!" the man begged, sobbing uncontrollably.

Manoj grabbed him by the collar and dragged him to the open trunk. He forced the man to look inside at the terrified Swati.

"There. Now you've seen it. Haven't you?" Manoj hissed.

Swati stared at the man with wide, desperate eyes, silently begging him to do something, anything.

"Please… It's empty…the trunk…nothing… I swear… nothing…" the man whimpered, tears streaming down his face.

Kamlesh and Dilip snickered, enjoying the spectacle.

Manoj pulled a thin nylon rope from his pocket, looping it slowly around the man's neck. The man cried harder, babbling incoherently.

"My son has exams tomorrow… My mother is sick… Please… please…" he wept, his voice trembling with desperation.

Manoj tugged the rope tighter, cutting off the man's pleas. The man gasped for air, his eyes bulging, red and frantic, locking onto Swati's. For a fleeting moment, Swati thought she saw something deeper than fear in his gaze. His eyes, desperate and unblinking, seemed to accuse her. To blame her. As though, in his final moments, he had decided that this was her fault—that her very presence, her helplessness, was the reason he was being killed.

Swati froze, her struggling ceasing entirely. A chill crept over her as the man's silent curse seemed to root itself in her soul. She wanted to scream, to beg for his forgiveness, but no words came. She could only watch as the light in his eyes flickered and died, leaving her with a haunting emptiness that felt heavier than the air around her.

"Shhh… quiet now," Manoj whispered to her, letting the man's body slump forward into the trunk with a dull *thud*.

Kamlesh dragged the lifeless body off the road, dumping it carelessly in the field. Dilip kicked the fallen Vespa into the ditch and picked up two guavas that had rolled out of the man's bag.

"Sweet," Dilip muttered, biting into a guava as he climbed back into the car.

Manoj lit another cigarette, the flame from his lighter briefly illuminating his cold, remorseless face.

The car engine roared to life again, and the Verna disappeared down the lonely road, leaving behind nothing but a silent jungle and the lifeless man—a forgotten casualty in the dark.

The car cruised for another hour or two, cutting through the oppressive silence of the night. Streetlights had long vanished, replaced by towering trees that loomed over the narrow road. The last traces of human presence were left behind, and now the vehicle pierced through the dense, silent jungle.

In the dark trunk, Swati's mind raced desperately, searching for any way out of the nightmare that awaited her. She had tried everything to wriggle free from the ropes that bound her, her wrists raw from the effort. The large tennis ball forced into her mouth, held tight with layers of tape, was a constant source of agony. Her teeth dug into the rubber, but it was unyielding. Her jaw muscles ached, stretched to their limit, while saliva pooled in her mouth, drooling uncontrollably onto her chin. Her eyes, swollen with tears, burned from exhaustion and despair.

In the darkest corners of her mind, a flicker of faith struggled to stay alive. *Om Vigneshwaraya Namaha... Om Gan Ganpataye Namah...* she chanted silently in her mind, repeating the name of Lord Ganesha over and over, clinging to it like a lifeline. The words were her shield against the encroaching darkness, her desperate plea for strength and deliverance. Yet, as the chant echoed within her, doubt crept in—was anyone even listening? Or was this, too, just another empty whisper in a cruel, indifferent universe?

Could they be reasoned with? Swati's thoughts spun wildly, grasping at the faintest threads of hope. Maybe—just maybe— they'd let her go if she stopped resisting. If she turned friendly, compliant. But would they really? Could she even trust such monsters to show mercy?

Her mind leaped to another idea: isolate one of them. Convince him to protect her. But which one? She began replaying what little she had seen of them in her mind, trying to read their faces, their movements, their words. Manoj—the leader—seemed too cruel, his anger and control unshakable. Kamlesh, with his mocking laughter, was no better; there was nothing human left in his eyes. Then there was Dilip, the one who was in the trunk with her. He had touched her, violated her, but maybe his proximity meant he was the weakest link. Maybe, just maybe, she could manipulate him.

Her thoughts churned, dark and desperate, as she tried to calculate her next move. The air in the trunk felt suffocating now, heavy with her fear and the sick anticipation of what was to come. Every bump in the road sent jolts through her body as fear clutched her heart, tightening with every mile.

Inside the car, Kamlesh and Dilip noisily munched on stolen guava, their carefree laughter a stark contrast to the heavy darkness outside. Manoj sat by the open window, puffing on a Goldflake cigarette, the glowing ember briefly illuminating his sharp features.

A weathered sign loomed ahead in the headlights: *Khandav*. The blood-red letters were smeared crudely across its surface, and beneath them, a black cross was scratched violently, like a final warning to turn back.

Manoj straightened in his seat. "Stop the car," he barked. Dilip hit the brakes with a screech, jerking the vehicle to a halt.

Manoj pointed at the dirt trail that branched off from the main road, disappearing into the dense jungle. "There. Let's go there."

Dilip frowned but followed the order, veering off the tar road and into the muddy path. "We'll go two, three kilometers in, find a nice spot, have some fun, and dump her. Then we sell the car and vanish," Manoj said.

Kamlesh chuckled from the back seat. "The girl's a gem, man. Shouldn't we keep her for a couple of days, have some real fun?"

Manoj turned to him with a sneer. "Listen to this fucking Romeo. What's next? You want to marry her?"

Both Manoj and Dilip snickered. Kamlesh, undeterred, took a swig from the bottle stashed under the seat. The jungle thickened around them as the dirt trail twisted deeper into the woods. The moon hung low in the sky, casting a cold, blue glow over the forest floor, but the dense canopy swallowed much of the light. Only the car's headlights sliced through the fog, illuminating the road ahead.

Dilip pulled over beneath a large, looming tree. "Perfect," he muttered, switching off the engine.

Manoj climbed out, unzipping to take a piss by the roadside. Kamlesh stumbled to the back, yanked open the trunk, and grinned at the terrified girl huddled inside. Her eyes were wide with fear, her breath coming in ragged bursts through the gag. Kamlesh hoisted her over his shoulder, giving her a sharp slap on the butt. "Let's dance, sweetheart," he slurred.

In the glow of the headlights, he set her down and spun her clumsily in a mock tango. Her tied legs made her movements awkward, her body jerking as she tried to keep her balance. Kamlesh's leering grin widened as her breasts jiggled with every desperate hop. She stumbled and fell hard onto the hood of the car before sliding limply to the ground.

"Oops! Sorry, babe," Kamlesh cackled, wiping his nose with the back of his hand.

Dilip stepped out of the car, his amused expression faltering as his gaze fixed on the road ahead. He stiffened. "Oi… something's there."

Manoj zipped up, turning toward the road. A dark figure stood in the middle of the path, motionless and silent.

"Who the fuck is that?" Kamlesh asked, squinting.

Manoj narrowed his eyes. "What the fuck…"

The girl whimpered, trying to hop back toward the car, but the ropes around her legs made every movement painfully slow. Her muffled cries barely broke the suffocating silence.

Dilip pulled out his knife, his hand trembling slightly. "This isn't right, man."

Manoj clicked the revolver's cylinder into place. "You want to play, motherfucker?" he growled, aiming at the figure.

They took cautious steps forward, but before they could act, the figure dropped onto all fours. Its head tilted sharply, sniffing the air like a beast before letting out a guttural growl. Then it scuttled toward the road's edge, its movements jerky and insect-like, vanishing into the undergrowth.

"What the fuck!" Kamlesh shouted, stumbling backward.

"Don't lose sight!" Manoj barked, charging forward.

Dilip sprinted ahead of them, his knife glinting under the moonlight. But when they reached the edge of the forest, there was nothing—just darkness and the silent menace of the trees.

They stood still, their breaths shallow and quick. "What now?" Dilip whispered.

"Shit, we need to get out of here," Manoj muttered. They turned back toward the road, their nerves on edge.

The girl, still hopping in the headlights, looked ridiculous. Even in the tense moment, Manoj smirked. "Fucking circus act."

But then the car roared to life, its engine revving loudly, shattering the oppressive silence of the jungle. The girl turned toward the vehicle, her eyes wide with panic as she hopped frantically, trying to get closer.

"How the fuck did it get in the car? Keys! Where the fuck are the keys?" Manoj shouted, his voice cracking with anger and fear.

Dilip froze, his face pale. "Weren't you supposed to have them?"

The car accelerated toward them, its headlights blazing like predatory eyes. The girl stumbled forward, banging her head against the driver's side window in desperation, her muffled screams barely audible. But the vehicle sped up, and she tumbled to the ground, rolling into the dirt.

Kamlesh, too drunk to comprehend what was happening, staggered directly into the car's path. The vehicle struck him with a sickening thud, sending his body flying through the air. He landed hard by the roadside, his limbs twisted unnaturally, blood pooling beneath his head as he groaned weakly.

The car screeched to a halt nearby. For a moment, all was still. Then, the sound of a car door opening echoed in the air, followed by the hollow *click* of it shutting.

Manoj and Dilip stared, their breaths shallow and uneven, but they couldn't see the driver.

From behind the trees, Manoj and Dilip watched the scene unfold. "What now?" Dilip whispered, his voice trembling.

Manoj shook his head, gesturing for him to stay hidden. Kamlesh lay sprawled on the ground, struggling to stand but collapsing again with a weak moan.

A shadow emerged from the forest. It crouched by Kamlesh, grabbing his leg. The figure turned to Manoj and Dilip, fixing them with a chilling stare.

Manoj froze, unable to pull the trigger. The shadow dragged Kamlesh into the jungle effortlessly. Kamlesh's desperate screams faded into the night.

Manoj and Dilip bolted toward the car, yanking at the doors, but they were locked. Panic gripped them both as they turned and ran down the road, their breaths ragged and uneven.

The girl, still bound, tried to follow, hopping pathetically after them. But halfway there, she stopped, glancing back at the car, then turned and started hopping toward it.

Manoj and Dilip skidded to a halt when they saw the figure standing ahead of them on the road.

"How the fuck did it get there?" Dilip whispered, his voice cracking with fear.

"Motherfucker!" Dilip screamed, charging toward the shadow with his knife raised.

The figure didn't move as Dilip lunged. It caught him mid-air and slammed him into the ground with bone-cracking force. The back of Dilip's head smashed into a stone, and he let out a gurgling noise before falling limp.

The shadow's eyes remained locked on Manoj, who stood paralyzed with fear. It dipped its hand into Dilip's blood, tasted it, and smiled.

"BANG!" Manoj fired a shot, but the figure disappeared into the forest.

Manoj sprinted back to the car, panting. The girl sat in the headlights, cutting through her ropes with the knife Kamlesh had dropped. She spat out the tennis ball, her face slick with saliva, and gasped for air.

Manoj climbed onto the car's roof, revolver in hand, scanning the darkness in every direction. The girl stood below him, clutching the knife, unsure whether he would shoot her.

Manoj ignored her completely. His eyes darted around the silent jungle, oblivious to her presence.

Then, above him, the branch moved. The shadow crawled along it, slithering silently. The girl froze in terror, her eyes wide with fear.

Manoj finally looked at her—then up.

Too late.

The figure dropped from the branch with a heavy thud.

"BANG!" The bullet missed.

The girl fell backward in shock, landing hard on the road. Blood dripped onto the windshield, obscuring her view. She could not see what happened on the roof. She tightened grip on knife in her hand.

She lay still, watching as a hand slid slowly over the glass. The shadow crawled onto the hood, its blood-filled eyes locking onto hers. She pointed the knife, her hands trembling with fear.

The face came into view—grinning, feral. It was Maruti.

He leaped, and the girl's scream echoed through the jungle.

Search for Professor

"Why, sometimes I've believed as many
as six impossible things before breakfast."

– Through the looking glass

Her reputation preceded her everywhere. The framed photo of Savarkar and the smaller frame of Asaram Bapu on the tabletop were enough to suggest she wouldn't be welcomed here. Yet, surprisingly, Shukla Madam, the Head of the Botany Department, was quite helpful. Maybe, Maya thought, the ongoing political climate had intensified prejudices too much. Or perhaps this was just an exception.

Anjali Shukla was in her early fifties, a small-framed woman with glasses perched on the bridge of her nose and a grey saree that matched her steel-gray hair. She sat in a large chair behind a glass table, her academic achievements framed proudly on the wall. Yet Maya couldn't ignore the mocking presence of Asaram's photo on the desk. *Education is supposed to lift people out of superstition and false beliefs,* she thought with quiet disdain. *But weaker minds will always seek refuge in them.*

"It's a tragedy to lose someone of Vikram's stature. The whole staff and students are still in shock," Shukla said, her voice carrying a note of genuine sorrow.

"Yes, I can hardly believe it myself," Maya replied. "I interviewed him once, before he published his famous book." She leaned forward, her tone shifting to feigned curiosity. "Please, tell me anything you know about him—especially about his last few days. I'm writing a piece on him for an upcoming magazine."

Shukla's gaze softened. "He was a deeply scientific person, a staunch atheist. I often told him to put his faith in God, but he'd laugh it off. We had many debates on the subject." She sighed, a faint smile tugging at her lips. "Then something happened. About ten or eleven months ago, he took the MSc Botany students on a field trip to the Western Ghats. When he came back... he was a different man. Confused, delusional. Nobody knows what happened. The students said he saw a ghost in the jungle." Shukla paused, her expression clouded with worry.

"A ghost?" Maya's brows knitted together. "Did the police try to find out more?"

"They registered him as a missing person, issued some advisories, and pretended to investigate. You know how it works." Shukla's voice held a bitter edge. "But the strangest part? Vikram had started going to temples, reading old scriptures, and discussing them with me. It was as if he was searching for something... beyond science." She hesitated, her eyes glistening with unspoken sadness.

"Really? I can hardly believe it," Maya replied, jotting notes in her diary. *Something drastic must have happened to change him so completely. A staunchly religious person can turn to atheism with enough learning and skepticism, but the other way around? That was far less likely.* Freedom from religion carried a unique clarity, a perspective on society that seemed irreplaceable—especially in a country like India, where this freedom held profound meaning. *Why would someone choose to give that up for the chains of belief?*

"Yes," Shukla whispered. "One day, he told me he was a seeker of truth. And then... he was gone."

Maya looked up from her notes. "Does that mean he went back to the forest? To see the... ghost? Didn't anyone investigate that angle?"

"Perhaps he did go back, but who would bother to look? The police questioned some villagers in the area, but no one claimed to have seen him." Shukla's voice grew softer, almost wistful.

"Some say he might have become a saint in his search for truth. That's what the police like to believe, anyway."

Maya frowned. "Any dependents? Lover? Parents? I know he wasn't married."

Shukla tilted her head thoughtfully, a faint, almost wistful smile tugging at her lips. "He always claimed science was his one true love," she said, her tone carrying a hint of something left unsaid. "Though… sometimes, the heart finds connections in unexpected places." Her gaze lingered on Maya for a moment before adding, "He has a mother. All the proceeds from his book go to her. I can give you her address if you'd like to speak to her."

Shukla scribbled the address on a slip of paper and handed it to Maya, who thanked her before saying, "I'd also like to speak to some of the students, if that's alright."

Shukla's gaze lingered for a moment. "Of course," she replied, her tone carefully neutral but tinged with something more. "MSc Botany, second year—they're likely in the lab right now. You'll want to ask for Nasreen. She was… eh… close to Professor Vikram."

Maya caught the slight emphasis, her pen pausing mid-air. Shukla continued, her casual air feeling deliberate. "Nasreen was his pet student. Always eager to assist him with his research. I'm sure she'll have… unique insights." Shukla's gaze held Maya's for a moment longer, as though waiting for her to catch on. "You know, some students form… attachments to their professors. It's natural. Inspiring, even."

Maya pocketed the note, feeling a spark of anticipation. As she left the office, her mind whirled with questions. *What happened to Vikram in the jungle? What could make a man abandon his very beliefs?*

Nasreen looked effortlessly beautiful in her white lab coat, layered over a traditional salwar-kurta that hinted at her Kashmiri roots. The soft, pastel fabric complemented her porcelain skin, which seemed to glow under the sterile fluorescence of the botany lab. The room itself was a paradox of order and organic chaos—long workbenches lined with glass beakers, test tubes, and petri dishes, all neatly organized yet surrounded by scattered leaves, specimens, and open botanical books. A faint, earthy scent lingered in the air, as though the plants themselves breathed within the confines of the space.

Rows of shelves were filled with labeled jars containing preserved plant specimens, their pale, twisted forms suspended in amber liquid. Against one wall stood cabinets stocked with carefully labeled tools and microscopes, while large botanical diagrams and hand-drawn sketches of plant anatomy adorned the other walls, adding a touch of vibrancy to the otherwise clinical setting. The soft hum of an overhead fan blended with the faint rustling of leaves from a small potted plant near the window, creating a subtle rhythm that underscored the room's quiet energy.

Maya found herself acutely aware of her surroundings, her senses heightening as she absorbed both the lab's atmosphere and Nasreen's quiet elegance. The combination made her feel as though she'd stepped into another world—one that was surreal and disarming.

Maya had long suspected her sexuality, but one look at Nasreen seemed to confirm it. The sharpness of her jawline, the gentle curve of her lips, and the effortless grace with which she moved held an allure Maya couldn't ignore. It was as if the air itself shifted when Nasreen spoke or moved, drawing Maya closer with every passing moment. Perhaps this was why her friends, like Nikhil Gaikwad, had always been so frustrated with her disinterest in men. She'd brushed off every advance, unconsciously waiting for a moment like this—meeting someone who made her heart quicken and her thoughts falter.

No wonder Vikram might have fallen for her, if he did as Shukla hinted, Maya thought. *Anyone would.*

"So, you're planning to meet Sir's mother?" Nasreen asked, her voice soft yet steady, pulling Maya back to the present. They had been talking for fifteen minutes just outside the lab, during which Nasreen had shared details of the fateful field trip with Vikram.

Maya's eyes drifted downward. Nasreen's lips—pink, full, effortless—moved as she spoke, yet Maya barely registered the words. There was something magnetic about them, something that stirred a forgotten memory.

Winter. She must have been in the seventh standard. She and Geeta had curled up together on a floor mattress, wrapped in a thick quilt, watching an old romantic movie on TV. The air was cold, their breaths little puffs of mist in the dim glow of the screen. They had been innocent, curious, untouched by the weight of years.

"Have you ever kissed anyone?" Geeta had whispered.

Maya had shaken her head. A nervous giggle, a moment's hesitation, and then, without thinking, she had leaned in. Just a small, soft kiss. Innocent. Fleeting. A secret they had carried between them, giggling about it all night.

It had felt beautiful. Strange, yet beautiful.

And it had been her first. And last.

After Geeta's death, Maya had never looked at anyone's lips the way she was staring now. A strange urge stirred within her, something unspoken, something she had long buried. The memory of that night flickered in her mind, overlapping with the present. Her stare lingered—too long.

Nasreen seemed to notice.

"Yes, maybe I'll go directly from here," Maya replied, trying to steady her voice, her gaze locked on Nasreen's deep, expressive eyes.

Nasreen tilted her head thoughtfully, her brows knitting in a way that only made her more captivating. "Can you wait, maybe another hour? I'll finish my practical and join you. It's been a while since I last saw Ma."

The suggestion sent a thrill through Maya, and she struggled to keep her composure. "Sure…umm. I'll wait in the cafeteria," she said, her words slightly unsteady.

Nasreen smiled, her eyes twinkling with quiet charm. "Take a right when you leave the department. I'll see you there."

As Nasreen turned and hurried back into the lab, Maya stood rooted in place, her gaze following the gentle sway of Nasreen's form. Just before disappearing, Nasreen glanced over her shoulder, catching Maya's lingering look. She offered a warm, knowing smile that sent Maya's heart racing.

A blush crept up Maya's cheeks as Nasreen vanished down the corridor. Her pulse quickened, anticipation filling her chest. Waiting in the cafeteria suddenly didn't feel like a chore—it felt like the beginning of something.

The trip to Vikram's house was a short one. Maya and Nasreen sat together in the rickshaw, the narrow seat forcing their shoulders to brush against each other every time the vehicle jolted over a pothole. The ride took about twenty minutes, but for Maya, it was the most exciting journey she had taken in a long time.

Sitting next to Nasreen, talking to her, watching her—it felt strangely electrifying. Every small gesture, every flicker of her fingers, every slight movement of her lips held an unspoken allure.

"Where are you from?" Maya asked, her voice casual, but her curiosity genuine.

"Ah... Mumbai," Nasreen replied smoothly.

Maya turned her head slightly, her eyes narrowing. That answer didn't seem quite right.

Nasreen noticed. A smirk played on her lips before she corrected herself, "Originally, Kashmir."

Maya's expression still held a question, as if expecting more. She was intrigued by Nasreen's openness—how effortlessly she shifted between identities, how she didn't hesitate in reshaping her story depending on the situation.

Nasreen had been born in Kashmir but raised in Delhi. Her father, a merchant, was a deeply religious man, and so was her mother. She had grown up in a happy and loving home, shielded from the outside world—until the world changed. Slowly, the political tides had shifted, and her community, like so many others, found itself being pushed aside, forced into the margins of society. Even in cities like Mumbai, the divide was apparent, choices stark.

There were two paths: stand your ground, become a part of the crowd, seek strength in numbers, and embrace your identity unapologetically—or discard it entirely. Blend in. Become something else.

Nasreen had chosen the latter.

And her family had never opposed her. They had only wanted her to be happy.

With sharp wits, striking beauty, and an unshakable free-spirited nature, Nasreen had navigated her life like a chessboard, knowing exactly when to advance, when to retreat, and when to let things slide.

"It's funny, really," she said suddenly, her voice laced with irony. "You spend half your life proving you belong, and the other half proving you're different. But in the end, no one really cares."

Maya let out a laugh—a genuine, unrestrained laugh, something rare for her these days.

"It's true… no one fucking cares…" she echoed.

But they did. The world, the people in it—they cared more than they ever admitted. They formed opinions before even speaking to you. Your name, your surname, your color, your breed—everything mattered. You can joke about it or casually laughed it off. But, opinions and prejudices had roots, deep and tangled, not easily shaken away.

Both Nasreen and Maya knew it.

The laughter faded, but a quiet understanding lingered between them as the rickshaw rattled to a stop in front of an isolated bungalow, its walls aged and silent, holding secrets of their own.

"That trip! It completely changed my Vikram!" Vikram's mother's voice trembled as tears welled in her eyes, her grief raw and unhidden. Nasreen sat close beside her, holding her hand in quiet support, as though she had done this countless times before. Maya observed the ease with which Nasreen comforted her, and a flicker of Shukla Madam's words echoed in her mind: *"Some students form… attachments to their professors."* Could this be what Shukla had hinted at?

Maya couldn't ignore the possibilities. Vikram was more than twice Nasreen's age, but his charisma and intellect could easily inspire admiration—or perhaps something deeper. Nasreen's closeness to "Ma" seemed unusually intimate, and Maya couldn't help but wonder if their connection went beyond a mere teacher-student bond. *Did they have a relationship?* The thought sent a pang of jealousy through her, an emotion so alien it left her momentarily disoriented. *Jealous of a missing professor?* The absurdity of it made her cheeks flush, but the feeling lingered.

"He became so… religious," Ma continued, wiping her tears. "He told me he met Shyam in the jungle." Her voice broke, and Nasreen squeezed her hand comfortingly. Maya, having already heard about the field trip from Nasreen, leaned in, intrigued by this mention of Shyam.

"What happened to Shyam, if I may ask?" Maya asked gently.

For a moment, Ma was silent, a haunted look in her eyes. The weight of losing both sons—one to death and the other to disappearance—was palpable. Though Vikram's best-selling book's proceeds were sent to her, it was clear that no amount of money could ease her pain.

"There was an accident," Ma said finally, her voice barely above a whisper. "Vikram was around thirty, and Shyam was just eighteen. Vikram was driving." She paused, her gaze distant. "It was nighttime, and a truck was parked on the road with no lights. They crashed into it from behind. Shyam… he died on the spot. Vikram was in the hospital for over a month." Ma's eyes drifted to the window, as if staring into the past. Then, seeming to shake herself free of the memory, she stood abruptly. "Let me make you some tea."

Maya sensed that Ma needed a break from the questions, but her curiosity was relentless. "I'm so sorry for your loss," she said softly. "May I see Vikram's room?"

Ma nodded. "Go ahead. It's upstairs. Nasreen, could you show her the way?"

Nasreen pointed toward the stairs but then followed Ma into the kitchen, leaving Maya to explore Vikram's room alone.

The room was a treasure trove of Vikram's intellectual pursuits, filled with books on various subjects that spoke to his unquenchable curiosity. Among them, recent titles on ghosts and psychology lay scattered across his desk, interspersed with academic texts and papers. A shelf lined with religious scriptures—*Bhagavad Gita, Quran,* even a *Mormon Bible*—caught Maya's attention. But what stood out the most were the ancient, timeworn tomes stacked in a corner, their leather bindings cracked with age. Titles like *The Key of Solomon, De Occulta Philosophia,* and *The Grand Grimoire* whispered of arcane knowledge. Books on spirits, demonology, and forgotten rituals exuded an eerie presence, their faded pages marked with cryptic annotations in the margins. The air in the room seemed heavier around them, as if centuries of forbidden knowledge had seeped into their very fabric.

She scanned the shelves and flipped through a few books, searching for notes or markings, but nothing stood out. Frustrated, she opened a desk drawer and rifled through its contents until she found a neatly kept box with a piece of tape labeled "Logs." Inside were several SD memory cards, each marked with a date. Her pulse quickened as she picked up the most recent one. Glancing around to ensure no one was watching, she discreetly slipped it into her purse, along with a small blue diary filled with botanical notes.

When Maya returned downstairs, Nasreen had placed a tray with three cups of tea on the table. The three women sat together, sipping in silence until Maya broke it.

"Did you tell the police about the ghost incident?" she asked.

Ma nodded, her expression resigned. "Yes, but they only went through the motions. They questioned a few villagers near the jungle, but no one saw Vikram there. I've come to accept how they work," she added bitterly. "They have nothing to gain from this, so I don't expect much."

Her gaze grew distant as she continued, "If I weren't convinced that Vikram had become a saint and left everything behind, I would have hired a private investigator to search for him. But that accident—it changed him. It made him reject all he once believed. And then this… this encounter, whatever it was… it turned him back toward God."

Maya listened intently, her mind racing with questions. Ma's sorrow seemed tempered by an unyielding determination.

"Thank you for trusting me," Maya said, her voice steady. "I'll do my best to find him."

Ma nodded, her tone firm. "I believe you will. You have a purpose here—something to gain from finding him. And if you need anything, please let me know. I have more than enough money. I just want my boy to be found, even if he has turned into some kind of saint. I need to be sure."

They exchanged phone numbers, and Maya felt a sense of resolve settle within her. As she stood to leave, Nasreen reached out and gently placed a hand on hers.

"Where next?" Nasreen asked softly, her voice like a soothing balm after the weight of the conversation.

Maya looked at her, momentarily captivated by the warmth of Nasreen's touch. Her fingers lingered a fraction longer than necessary, her pulse quickening as their eyes met. For a brief, electric moment, the world seemed to fall away, leaving only the soft hum of the overhead fan and the faint scent of tea between them.

"Jungle," Maya finally replied, her voice quiet, almost hesitant. She withdrew her hand slowly, but the absence of Nasreen's touch left her feeling unsteady.

Nasreen smiled, her expression unreadable, and stepped back. "Be careful and Good luck," she said simply.

As Maya turned toward the door, she glanced back one last time. Nasreen stood by the table, her gaze following Maya, her posture relaxed but somehow expectant. Maya's chest tightened, a swirl of unfamiliar emotions rising within her—desire, curiosity, and a yearning she hadn't felt in years.

Her thoughts were a jumble as she stepped outside, the cool evening air hitting her skin. *Focus, Maya,* she told herself. *You're here to find answers, not… this.*

But as she walked away, she couldn't shake the image of Nasreen's knowing smile, and for the first time in years, the pursuit of truth felt like it might lead to something more than just answers.

Whispers in the Fog

"Not all who wander are lost, but some who vanish are never found."

– J R R Tolkien

Ravsaheb had once been the undisputed wrestling champion of Dongarwadi and the surrounding villages. Now in his early forties, he still carried the strength and pride of his youth, coaching the village boys in wrestling when he wasn't working in the fields. Tonight, he had stayed late on his farm, waiting for the power supply to finally come on so he could water his crops. With a spade slung over his shoulder, he began his walk back to the village as the last light of the sun sank behind the horizon.

The jungle surrounding Dongarwadi was alive with the hooting of monkeys, their cries echoing eerily from the trees. Ravsaheb paused at the edge of the village, peering into the thick shadows of the jungle. The hooting usually meant a predator was nearby, though his sharp eyes couldn't pick out anything yet. Faint strains of a Bollywood song drifted on the evening breeze, mingling with the earthy scent of the fields.

Not far from him, Shrikant, the village ironsmith, was crouched in the bushes, relieving himself. Like many in the village, who lacked proper toilet facilities, he came to the fields in the evenings. Hearing Ravsaheb's voice, he froze, afraid to make a sound.

"Who's there?" Ravsaheb called out, his gaze fixed on the darkness between the trees. He thought he saw a figure moving, silhouetted against the pale glow of the half-moon. He flicked on his torch and aimed the beam at the movement.

A young woman stepped slowly out of the shadows, her face partially illuminated by the light. She wore a shimmering party dress that clung to her figure, her big thighs exposed and inviting, her cleavage just visible. Her beauty was mesmerizing, almost surreal—an otherworldly presence in the jungle's gloom. Ravsaheb's pulse quickened, a mix of fear and primal desire coursing through him. He had heard tales of the jungle's strange allure, of how it drew people in, never to return. But he had never seen anything like this. If this was the jungle's seduction, it was hauntingly beautiful.

Swati Seth smiled and took a step closer, her movements slow and hypnotic, as if pulled from the pages of a dream. Ravsaheb stood frozen, transfixed, as she closed the distance. "Stop right there!" he called out, his voice unsteady. He raised his torch, letting the beam travel down her face to her bare legs. "Who are you? Do you need help?"

Her smile widened, an unsettling blend of warmth and coldness. Her eyes, glinting unnaturally, never wavered from his as she advanced, like a predator sizing up its prey. Ravsaheb's instincts screamed at him to run, but he was rooted to the spot, unable to break free from her gaze.

Unseen by Raosaheb, two more shadows emerged silently from the jungle behind him. One moved with a limp, its gait uneven, unnatural.

Shrikant's blood ran cold as recognition slammed into him.

It was Maruti.

Maruti, who had left the village weeks ago—to die.

He had walked away toward the jungle, speaking of an end, of relief, of never returning. And he hadn't. Not until now.

Shrikant clamped a hand over his mouth, stifling a gasp. The shock left him frozen, his mind struggling to process the impossible. Maruti should have been dead.

Yet, here he was.

Moving. Breathing. Changed.

Shrikant's wide, unblinking eyes remained locked on the nightmare unfolding before him.

Swati knelt before Ravsaheb, her face inches from his groin. A surge of wild, uncontrollable desire overtook him, clouding his thoughts. He looked down, but instead of anticipation, an icy dread crept into his chest. Something was horribly wrong. The girl wasn't offering pleasure—she was waiting, poised like a trap.

Ravsaheb instinctively turned, his torchlight cutting through the darkness, just as a heavy fist collided with his face. The force of the blow sent him staggering forward, his body crumpling onto Swati Seth's shoulder as she knelt in front of him. Her expression didn't change; she remained eerily calm, as if she'd been waiting for this moment. With unnatural ease, she stood, hoisting Ravsaheb onto her shoulder like a sack of grain.

The group melted into the shadows of the jungle, taking Ravsaheb with them. The eerie silence that followed was broken only by the faint rustling of leaves as they disappeared deeper into the trees.

Shrikant sat crouched in the bushes, his entire body trembling. He had held his breath for so long that his chest ached, his face flushed from the effort.

And then it happened.

A loud, unmistakable fart ripped through the stillness, betraying his presence.

Shrikant's heart stopped. His wide eyes darted toward the jungle, praying the sound hadn't carried too far. For a moment, nothing stirred. The oppressive silence resumed, but he could swear the trees themselves were watching him.

Terrified and humiliated, Shrikant clamped both hands over his mouth, holding back a whimper. He didn't dare move, his mind racing with the lingering image of Maruti's cold, dead eyes.

The jungle seemed to laugh at him in the form of a distant, mocking hoot from a monkey. Shrikant shivered and pressed himself deeper into the bush, vowing silently to never step near the forest's edge again.

Shrikant bolted toward the village, his legs trembling beneath him. He tore down the narrow, fog-choked path, barely aware of the cold biting into his skin. He burst through the door of his home, rushed to his room, and locked the door. Sliding down to the floor, he clutched a framed photo of Hanuman in his hands, chanting the Hanuman Chalisa under his breath, each word a fragile lifeline. Behind him, his large wife lay sprawled across the bed, her heavy snores filling the room like the grunts of a restless animal.

As dawn broke and the first rooster's crow pierced the stillness, Shrikant staggered to his feet. His wife stirred, blinking her eyes open to find him muttering by the door, his face pale, his gaze darting between the cracks in the wood as if something was watching from outside.

"What's wrong?" she asked, her voice thick with sleep.

He didn't reply, just stared at her for a long, hollow moment. Then, as though possessed, he yanked open the door and bolted from the house, his frantic steps echoing down the empty, mist-shrouded path toward Ramu Kaka's house.

There was time when Ramchandra Savarde now Ramu Kaka was a force of nature. In his prime, he was a wrestler, known for his iron grip and a voice that could shake the *akhada* (gym) as much as his blows. But strength alone wasn't enough—his sharp mind and ability to read people led him into local politics. From a fighter in the ring, he became a fighter for the people, rising to the position of village *sarpanch* (head).

He served with firmness but fairness, settling disputes, protecting the weak, and ensuring that his village ran smoothly.

But time spares no one.

His daughter married and moved to Mumbai. His son left for Pune, chasing city dreams. And when his wife passed away, something inside him quietly broke.

Now, at 75, Ramu Kaka was a different man. Calm. Quiet. Measured. He no longer wrestled men—he wrestled time itself. He saw the world with a tired but knowing gaze, observing more, interfering less. He had learned that people do what they will, regardless of wisdom or warnings.

Yet, despite his silence and solitude, his eyes never left the village. He still watched over his people, subtly ensuring their well-being. He had no grand illusions about life anymore—he was just waiting for his final call, knowing that in the grand scheme of things, men like him fade, and the world moves on.

But until that day came, Ramu Kaka remained. A relic of an older world, standing between the past and whatever was coming next.

Ramu was already awake, his wrinkled hands rubbing tobacco across his teeth. His house was silent, lonely—the kind of silence that had settled in ever since his wife passed and his sons moved to the city, leaving him behind to wander the ghostly, deserted village.

"Kaka… Kaka…!" Shrikant's voice trembled as he stumbled through the door.

Ramu looked up, frowning at the look of terror etched across Shrikant's face. "Catch your breath first. What's happened?"

"Raosaheb… the ghost… a ghost took him!"

Shrikant finally managed, his voice barely above a whisper. His hands trembled, his breath uneven.

Ramu Kaka's brow furrowed, deep lines of worry etching across his face. The shadows in the dimly lit room seemed to stretch, swallowing the corners, as if the very air had turned colder, heavier.

"Maruti was with them!" Shrikant blurted, his voice cracking.

Ramu Kaka's fingers tightened around his walking stick. "Maruti?"

"Yes! He's a ghost now!" Shrikant was almost hysterical.

A chill crawled up Ramu Kaka's spine. It was his fault.

Maruti had left the village cursing them all, announcing his intent to end his life. No one had taken him seriously. Not even Ramu Kaka.

But Maruti had done this before. He would stir up drama, threaten to kill himself, disappear for a few hours—then stumble back by evening, reeking of alcohol, the fire in his eyes burned out. It had become a habit, a cycle.

Only this time, he hadn't come back.

The villagers had whispered behind closed doors, debating what had happened. Some believed he had finally left for good, that he had walked out of their lives like so many before him. But no one truly believed he had done it.

Until now.

Now, Maruti had returned.

But not as a man.

A sudden, suffocating guilt gripped Ramu Kaka's chest. He should have stopped him. Like those countless other times.

He should have stood up, pulled him back—held him, maybe even hugged him.

Sometimes, it only takes one small gesture to stop a catastrophe.

It makes and breaks lives.

And Ramu Kaka had sat there and done nothing.

Maruti had walked with intent, and he had let him go.

And now Maruti was dead… or worse—

Not dead.

Ramu Kaka exhaled slowly, his jaw tightening. Wordlessly, he slipped on his glasses, his expression unreadable.

"Show me where it happened," he said, his voice low, steady. Shrikant swallowed hard and nodded.

They walked in silence through the empty village streets. The fog hung thick, muffling the sounds of the waking village. Somewhere in the distance, a cow's low groan broke the stillness, but no lights showed in the windows. Only the looming mountain beyond, half-shrouded by the thick mist, cast an eerie shadow over the path.

Shrikant led him to a patch of land just outside the village where the incident had supposedly taken place. "Here," he whispered, pointing to a darkened spot on the ground. A single spade lay abandoned nearby, its handle wet with dew. Ramu scanned the area, but the silence pressed in around them, thicker and heavier than before.

"Let's go to Ravsaheb's house," Ramu finally muttered, as if speaking any louder would summon something lurking in the mist. He cast a wary glance around, skeptical yet uneasy. "You might've been seeing things. Did you drink last night?"

But Shrikant shook his head vehemently, his face drained of color. Just then, the shadow of a figure materialized through the fog—a dark silhouette gliding toward them with an unnatural stillness. Both men froze, breathless, until the figure drew closer, revealing itself as Baburao on his moped, his engine silent in the thick air.

"Where were you so early?" Ramu asked, his voice steadier than he felt.

"Had work at the district office. Stayed the night there and came back early," Baburao replied, eyeing their wary expressions. "What's going on?"

"Come with us to Ravsaheb's house," Ramu said, voice low. He picked up the spade and climbed onto the back of Baburao's moped. Shrikant scrambled on as well, his hands clutching Baburao's shoulders with white-knuckled fear.

Ravsaheb's wife confirmed he hadn't returned from the fields, and Ramu showed her the spade. "Is this yours?"

She nodded, her face pale. "What happened?" she whispered, her eyes darting to the shadows lingering just beyond the doorway.

Before Ramu could explain, Shrikant blurted out, "Ravsaheb... he was taken... by a ghost!"

Ramu shot him a glare, hissing, "Quiet, you fool! We don't know that yet." But the woman's face had already gone slack with terror, her eyes welling with tears.

"Stop crying, woman!" Ramu barked, though his own voice shook slightly. "We'll find out what happened. Shrikant, go get Ganpati, Vilas, and Appa. Tell them it's urgent. And find Bandya—tell him to check Ravsaheb's field," he ordered, his words clipped.

Then, turning to Baburao, he muttered, "Fetch Bhairav."

The sun was beginning to rise, casting long, skeletal shadows across the ground as they prepared to search. But even in the light, the mist clung stubbornly to the earth, refusing to lift, as though it was hiding something that belonged in the dark.

The Dream

The recording played, filling Maya's dim, cluttered flat with haunting echoes. Frantic footsteps, desperate sobbing, and panicked screams spilled from the speakers, chilling the air. A young boy's trembling voice cut through the cacophony: *"What happened?"* A gasp followed—heavy, frantic—*"Ghost... Jungle!"* The breaths that came next were ragged and shallow, almost suffocating.

"Get in the bus... run... get out... quick!" commanded a voice, sharp with urgency. Maya felt the tension bleed from the recording, almost as if she were there. A rush of footsteps thundered, bodies jostling in chaos, and then the bus engine roared to life, its rumble slicing through the noise. *"Run!"* someone shouted, unmistakably Baburao, Maya guessed. The bus jolted forward, its tires crunching over uneven ground, but a distant scream pierced the clamor: *"Stop! Stop! Here!"*

Then silence. The bus groaned to a halt, its mechanical hum dying like a beast expiring in the fog.

Maya sat cross-legged on her bed, the pale glow of her laptop illuminating her face. Her one-bedroom flat felt suffocating, its disheveled state mirroring the chaos in her mind. She slipped the SD card from the laptop and reached for the next, her hands steady despite the tension mounting in her chest. She inserted the card and opened the single audio file.

Vikram's voice crackled to life, low and taut, as though he were confiding in the shadows.

"Day 25th of June," he began, his tone threaded with frustration. *"This is Vikram Jadhav. I have tried everything… spirituality, meditation, prayer. I went to temples, followed every path a good devotee should. But there are no answers."* He exhaled heavily, the sound weighted with despair. *"I saw what happened to my brother, and as a seeker of truth, I need to understand… to find out how."*

Maya leaned in closer, her pulse quickening.

"Hallucinations, maybe… but it was so real." He paused, his voice dropping to a whisper. *"Something is there in that place. Something in the ground, maybe? Physical or magnetic? Or perhaps… something alive…"* His words trailed off, as if even he doubted his thoughts. *"There's something hidden in that jungle."*

The room seemed to close in on her as Vikram's voice filled the air.

"Pheromones," he continued, his voice more measured. *"Secreted by insects, plants. They change behavior in creatures, draw animals in, control them. Even humans respond to pheromones. But… why only under the full moon? Like a werewolf? Or maybe… something that blooms? A periodic flower?"*

His tone softened into a barely audible murmur. *"Why wasn't Baburao affected? Maybe it only works on some people. Could someone be… immune to ghosts?"* He let out a dry, bitter chuckle. *"Are there real spirits? Are ghosts real? Well, I saw one for sure!"*

His voice wavered, laced with both conviction and lingering doubt, as if he couldn't quite bring himself to believe his own words.

After a long silence, his voice grew firm again. *"I've been distracted too long. It's time to find the truth. I'm leaving tomorrow. Over and out."*

The recording clicked off, and Maya's flat fell into silence once more. She stared at the screen, her mind racing to piece together the fragments of Vikram's last days. Her hands trembled as she reached for her phone and sent a quick message to Nilesh:

"I think I know where Vikram went. I'm going after him. I may be out of coverage for a few days."

Closing her eyes, she tried to make sense of it all—pheromones, full moons, immunity to ghosts. The cryptic words lingered in her thoughts as her exhaustion pulled her into a fitful sleep.

She was in the jungle. The air shimmered with a golden hue, thick with an intoxicating floral scent. Each step she took seemed to pull her deeper into its magic, her surroundings pulsating with a surreal energy. A mantis emerged from the shadows, its body glowing with iridescent hues that shifted like a living rainbow.

The insect turned its prism-like eyes toward her, tilting its head curiously. Its gaze was unsettlingly intelligent, almost amused. Without warning, the mantis emitted a burst of shimmering particles that floated in the air like ethereal dust. Maya inhaled instinctively, the sharp sweetness filling her lungs and flooding her senses with euphoria.

Nearby, a vibrant flower suddenly exploded, sending fragments of light and color spiraling through the air. In its place stood Nasreen, cloaked in a semi-transparent silk dress that clung to her body like water. She exuded an aura of seduction and mystery, her dark eyes glinting with something both inviting and unknowable.

Maya felt an irresistible pull, her heart pounding as she stepped closer. Nasreen's lips parted, their faces inches apart, but the spell shattered as something horrifying emerged. From Nasreen's mouth crawled a monstrous spider, its legs twitching, its glistening body filling the space where her tongue should have been.

Maya gasped, recoiling in terror, and the dream dissolved into a swirl of darkness.

Maya jolted awake, her heart hammering in her chest as sunlight streamed through the window. Disoriented, she reached for her phone, blinking at the multiple missed calls from Nasreen.

Her attention caught on a message:

"Tried calling you. It was somewhere in the jungle at the above location. Find Baburao; he knows the forest in that area. But honestly, there's nothing there except jungle. Do you think he went back? Call me in the evening. Take care."

Maya stared at the text, her pulse still racing from the dream. Her mind churned with possibilities as she reread Nasreen's message, wondering if the location held the answers she sought—or the truth Vikram had been chasing.

The Seeker of Truth

"We live, as we dream—alone."

– Heart of Darkness

Vikram stepped off the bus in Dongarwadi, his boots crunching against the dusty roadside. He scanned his surroundings, spotting a villager leaning against a small shop. "Do you know where I can find Baburao?" he asked, adjusting the heavy trekking bag slung over his shoulder.

The man squinted, his brow furrowing. "Baburao? Hmm… Babu…"

"The one with the forest department," Vikram clarified.

The villager's face lit up with recognition. "Ah, Babya Kamble! Follow that road," he said, pointing toward a dirt path leading away from the village, "across from the main galli. You'll see a small cluster of houses—that's where he stays."

Vikram nodded his thanks, setting off in the direction indicated.

Maharashtra might have been one of India's most progressive states, but villages like Dongarwadi still bore the scars of a caste system ingrained over centuries. Ancient lines of segregation remained, with each caste occupying its designated *'galli.'* Those deemed lowest in the hierarchy lived just outside the village in isolated *bastis.* Though laws had chipped away at these divisions, the biases lingered, etched into daily life. Vikram, no stranger to these divides, tightened his grip on the strap of his bag and walked on, aware of the villager's faintly amused gaze following him.

The house was small but tidy, with a modest courtyard shaded by a *neem* tree. Inside, Vikram sat on a low wooden stool, cradling the steaming cup of tea Baburao had handed him. The walls bore few adornments, save for a statue of Buddha and a photograph of Dr. Babasaheb Ambedkar in a corner, their silent presence offering a glimpse into Baburao's beliefs.

Baburao, a wiry man in his late fifties, leaned against the doorframe, his sharp eyes fixed on Vikram with a mix of curiosity and disbelief. "You're crazy to come back here," he said, shaking his head.

Vikram met his gaze, his voice calm but firm. "I need to find the truth. I don't believe in ghosts, Baburao. And neither should you."

Baburao Kamble was born into a humble yet loving family. His father, a bus driver in another district, spent most of his days on the road, while his mother sold vegetables in the local market to make ends meet. Despite their struggles, their home was filled with warmth and resilience.

A staunch Ambedkarite, Baburao's father kept him away from religion and superstitions, raising him with the ideals of rationality and self-respect. Baburao was an average student, but he harbored a quiet determination. However, when he moved to the city for college, reality struck hard. The weight of societal prejudice and bias chipped away at his already fragile confidence. His grades suffered, and he withdrew into himself.

Then came the diagnosis. A tumor had begun growing in Baburao's brain, an invisible enemy eating away at his future. The news devastated his parents. His father, who had fought the world for his son, now found himself powerless against fate. His mother, unable to bear the shock, passed away, leaving Baburao with a guilt that would never truly leave him.

Despite the medical uncertainty, Baburao fought on. His father remained his anchor, pushing him forward when his own resolve wavered. After years of struggle, Baburao not only got cured but also secured a job in the forest department, a place where he could escape the suffocating weight of society and find solace in the vast, indifferent wilderness. His father, proud but weary, passed away last year of old age, knowing his son had made something of himself.

Now, Baburao was alone. He never married, never even considered it. Perhaps the years of loss had built an invisible wall around him, or perhaps solitude was the only way he knew to exist. The jungle became his companion, its silence more comforting than the noise of the world he had left behind.

But then came the whispers. The stories. The things people saw in the jungle.

For years, Baburao had dismissed such tales as superstitions, nothing more than the exaggerated fears of simple folk. He had followed his father's teachings, never truly bowing to any god, never surrendering to blind faith. But in the last year, something had changed.

There were nights when the jungle felt too quiet, yet he could hear something just beyond the edge of perception—voices in the wind, murmurs between the trees. There were times when he thought he saw shadows that moved when nothing else did. The ghost stories he had once mocked started creeping into his mind, settling into the cracks of his reason.

Slowly, he felt something shift within him. He was no longer sure of what was real and what wasn't. Doubt had seeped into his thoughts like an infection. He still wouldn't call it faith, but in those fleeting moments of fear, he found himself bowing his head—not to a god, but to something unknown. He had never believed before. But now, belief—or something close to it—had begun to take root.

Baburao snorted, though his expression softened slightly. "Look, I don't know what to believe anymore. Too many people here have seen… things."

"Well, I've seen things too," Vikram replied, setting his cup down. "And I want to know what it was. Help me."

Baburao exhaled, rubbing his temples. "I know religion is a lie, but science isn't absolute truth either. The real truth—it's out there, waiting to be found."

"Then shouldn't we find it?" Vikram pressed.

"That's what I'm afraid of," Baburao murmured. "What if we do?"

He sighed, his eyes growing distant. "There have always been stories. Tales our grandfathers told to scare children—about the jungle calling to people, swallowing them up." He hesitated, lowering his voice. "But it's only in the last eight or ten months that these strange things have really started happening."

"Strange things?" Vikram leaned forward, intrigued.

Baburao nodded slowly, his voice barely above a whisper. "People say they've seen the dead—their loved ones. Fathers, mothers, sons, daughters. People they've lost… calling to them from the jungle. It's like the forest knows what's in their hearts, and it uses that to lure them in."

Vikram frowned. "And this only started recently?"

"Yes," Baburao replied. "Before that, it was just stories. Now, it feels… real."

Vikram's resolve hardened. "I need to see for myself again. I want to go into the jungle."

Baburao's eyes widened in alarm. "Are you out of your mind?"

"Maybe," Vikram admitted, his tone unwavering. "But I need you to come with me."

Baburao shook his head vehemently. "Why would I do that?"

"Why wouldn't you?" Vikram countered. "Don't you want to know what's really going on out there? Isn't that part of your job?"

"My job," Baburao snapped, frustration creeping into his voice, "is to look after the jungle, not chase ghosts. And if these so-called ghosts keep people away, the forest is probably better off. I don't care about finding some 'truth,' Vikram."

Vikram held his gaze, recognizing Baburao's unease. "Look, maybe we started off wrong. There has to be another way."

Baburao sighed, clearly exasperated. "The only way is for you to go back to wherever you came from."

Vikram leaned forward, his tone softening. "What if I paid you? Five thousand rupees for a trip into the jungle. I can go alone if I have to, but I'd rather have a guide."

Baburao's eyes narrowed as he considered. "Ten thousand," he said finally. "And I want half of it upfront."

"Seven," Vikram countered, pulling out his wallet. "Five now, two when we're back."

Baburao took the cash, glancing at it briefly before tucking it into his shirt pocket. "Fine," he muttered. "But you'll need to pay another three thousand to Bhairav."

"Bhairav?" Vikram raised an eyebrow. "Who's he?"

Baburao smirked. "You'll meet him soon enough. So, when do you want to go?"

Vikram didn't hesitate. "Now."

Bhairav was the local shaman, a man both revered and quietly feared by the villagers. His hut stood secluded, nestled close to the jungle about a kilometer and a half from Dongarwadi. Dense trees surrounded the area, their looming forms giving the place an air of watchful isolation. As Baburao parked his moped, Vikram dismounted, adjusting the straps of his heavy trekking bag. The narrow dirt road that led back to the village was a good 200 meters away—a reminder of just how remote this place truly was.

"Bhairav!" Baburao called, his voice cutting through the stillness.

The door creaked open, and a lean man emerged. He wore simple black pants and a white shirt, his round glasses perched delicately on a narrow nose, giving him a scholarly, almost unassuming appearance. If Vikram hadn't known better, he'd never have guessed this man was a shaman.

"What brings you here?" Bhairav asked, his tone clipped and wary as his sharp eyes flicked between Baburao and Vikram.

"This is Vikram," Baburao said, gesturing toward his companion. "A botany professor from Mumbai."

Vikram extended a hand, but Bhairav only nodded, his expression unreadable. "Come in, then," he muttered, stepping aside with a reluctant sigh.

Inside the dimly lit hut, Bhairav unrolled a woven carpet onto the floor. They sat in a loose circle around a jug of water and a single glass placed between them. As Baburao and Vikram recounted the strange events surrounding the jungle, Bhairav listened in silence, his expression darkening with every word.

They were nearly done when the door opened, and a woman entered, balancing a tray with three cups of tea. She was striking—a figure of quiet strength and elegance. Her simple sari clung to her toned frame, the drape falling just low enough to reveal a glimpse of her lean stomach and deep navel. Vikram noticed, against his will, the fluidity of her movements, as though every step and gesture was deliberate, almost feline.

"Savitri," Bhairav said without looking up, acknowledging her presence as she placed the tea before them. Baburao accepted his cup with a casual nod, while Vikram's focus lingered briefly on the woman before he quickly shifted his gaze back to Bhairav.

"What exactly do you want from me?" Bhairav asked, his voice sharper now, his gaze fixed on Vikram.

"We need to find Chendkai," Baburao said firmly.

At the mention of the name, Bhairav's face darkened, and a shadow seemed to pass over the room. "You're asking for trouble," he said, his voice barely above a whisper. "The jungle hasn't been the same for months. Going there now… it's not wise."

Vikram leaned forward, his tone urgent. "I don't believe in ghosts, Bhairav. I just want to understand what's really happening in that jungle. I'm offering three thousand rupees for your help."

Bhairav's gaze drifted toward the window, where the shadowed forest loomed like a living entity. "Three thousand won't buy safety in there," he said quietly, almost to himself.

"Come on, Bhairav," Baburao urged. "You know the jungle better than anyone."

Bhairav's fingers drummed nervously on the floor. "People have gone in and never come back," he murmured. "There are things in there…" His voice trailed off, his unease palpable. "You city folk think everything can be explained, but this… this is different."

"Five thousand," Vikram pressed, pulling out his wallet. "Half now, half when we're back."

After a long pause, Bhairav sighed heavily, his gaze locking with Vikram's. "Fine," he said. "But once we enter that jungle, remember this—you won't be in control. The jungle will decide whether you come out."

He called out, "Savitri, bring the box."

Savitri returned, carrying a small wooden box weathered with age. She moved with the same quiet grace, her dark eyes steady and unreadable. As she knelt to set the box on the floor, Vikram found his gaze drawn to her again—the curve of her lean arms, the faint sheen of sweat on her skin, the way her every movement seemed effortless yet deliberate.

Bhairav opened the box, revealing several small amulets wrapped in sacred threads. He murmured a soft incantation over them, his voice low and rhythmic, before handing one to Baburao and another to Vikram. The third he tied around his own wrist. "These tabeez will protect us," he said solemnly. "Keep them close. Do not take them off."

Vikram hesitated for a moment but followed Baburao's lead, tying the amulet around his wrist.

"These charms are three hundred rupees each," Bhairav added matter-of-factly. Vikram handed him six hundred rupees without complaint.

Reaching for his bag, Vikram began to prepare, but Bhairav stopped him with a raised hand. "Leave it. You'll need to move quickly and quietly. Carry only what's essential."

Reluctantly, Vikram opened his bag and pulled out his GoPro and audio recorder. He strapped the GoPro to his head, its faint beep as it powered on offering a small sense of security.

Bhairav stood, his eyes flicking toward the shadowed trees outside. "If we're doing this, we go now."

With a final glance at Savitri, who stood silently in the corner of the hut, Vikram followed Baburao and Bhairav out into the night. The jungle loomed ahead, its dense canopy seeming to stretch toward them like outstretched arms. As they crossed the threshold into the trees, Vikram couldn't shake the feeling that the jungle itself was watching, waiting.

"Date—Jan 10, 2020. First day at Dongarwadi. Check." Vikram replayed the recording in his headphones as he, Baburao, and Bhairav stepped out of the shaman's hut into the cool jungle air.

"Here I am with Baburao, a forest constable, and Bhairav, a local shaman, who has given me this supposedly protective *tabeez*," Vikram said with faint amusement into the recorder.

"It won't work," Bhairav suddenly interrupted, stopping in his tracks.

"What won't work?" Vikram asked, confused.

"The *tabeez*—it won't work if you don't believe in it. Faith is what gives it power," Bhairav replied, resuming his walk.

Vikram shrugged but couldn't entirely dismiss the shaman's words. "You mean belief makes it work? Like a placebo effect?"

Bhairav kept quiet. "Call it what you will," Baburao replied. "But belief is powerful. I've seen people die—not because they were poisoned, not because they were cursed, but because they believed they were cursed."

Bhairav ignored their talks and walked ahead. "It's true. There was a man in a nearby village. A quack told him someone had done black magic on him, and that his death was certain within a week. The poor guy went home, refused to eat, started losing his mind. By the seventh day, he was dead—without a scratch on him."

"Psychosomatic," Vikram said, his tone firm, but the unease in his expression betrayed him. "His belief killed him, not the so-called black magic."

Bhairav stopped to face him. "And just as belief can kill, it can protect. If you don't trust the *tabeez*, it's just a string around your wrist. But if you believe in it, it becomes a shield."

Vikram shrugged but couldn't dismiss Bhairav's words entirely. He had spent months observing the lives of believers, reading about their worlds of faith and rituals. While he remained a staunch skeptic—his brother's death only strengthening his disbelief—he understood how belief shaped their lives. *These believers have ecosystem of their own!* he wondered.

"Do you believe?" Vikram asked Baburao, who was walking slightly ahead.

"In what?" Baburao replied, looking over his shoulder.

"All of this—God, ghosts, magic?" Vikram gestured toward the thickening jungle around them.

Baburao nodded. "Yes, I believe. I haven't seen anything myself, but I believe they exist."

Vikram adjusted the recorder on his chest. "Where are we going exactly?"

"To Chendkai," Bhairav answered quietly.

"Who—or what—is Chendkai?" Vikram asked, intrigued.

Bhairav paused, as though deciding how much to say. "It's a story my grandfather told me, one not many people know," he said, his tone heavy with caution. "There was once a powerful *mantrik*—a mystic—who discovered a special plant in this jungle. With the right mixture, it could strip a person of their free will."

Vikram raised an eyebrow, glancing at Baburao, who remained quiet. Bhairav continued.

"The *mantrik*'s work was a closely guarded secret, known only to a few high-ranking officials. His potion became sought after by the powerful—for gathering enemy secrets, political manipulation, and even forcing women into submission." Bhairav's voice darkened as he spoke.

"Sounds like the *Dhatura* flower," Vikram interjected. "It's said to have similar properties, though those claims are exaggerated."

Bhairav gave him a quick glance. "This was far more potent and real. The *mantrik* also had a daughter, Chandrakka, a stunning beauty who assisted him in his rituals. Many men lusted after her but dared not act on their desires because of the *mantrik's* power and influence."

They walked in silence for a moment before Bhairav adjusted their path slightly. "We're close—just another kilometer or so," he said before continuing.

"Manipal, a minister of the king, often sought the *mantrik's* services. His son, Jaipal, was a vile man with dark ambitions. He wanted Chandrakka and decided to trick her father into submission. Jaipal laced sweets with potion bought by his father from same *mantrik*, and visited the *mantrik*'s house. He offered sweets, Chandrakka, who was fasting, pretended to eat the sweets out of politeness but kept them in the kitchen."

Bhairav's voice grew more intense as he spoke. "The *mantrik* ate the sweets and fell under Jaipal's control. Jaipal demanded to know the formula for the potion and all its secrets. The *mantrik* told him everything, speaking like a mindless puppet. Chandrakka realized they had been tricked but could only watch as Jaipal ordered her father to slit his own throat."

Vikram felt his stomach tighten. "And did he?" he asked softly.

"Yes," Bhairav said grimly. "Right in front of her. Then Jaipal and his men turned their attention to Chandrakka. They ordered her to undress."

Vikram felt a chill run down his spine. "What happened then?"

Bhairav hesitated, scanning the jungle ahead. "Chandrakka had no choice. She removed her clothes, pretending to submit. Jaipal took her into another room, locking the door. His men waited outside, assuming they would get their turn."

Baburao muttered under his breath, "Did she…?"

"She killed him! While Bhairav laid her down and mounted on her, Chandrakka found her chance," Bhairav said firmly. "Jaipal was thinking that she was under total control and so had kept his knife right next to her. She grabbed his knife, and slit his throat. Then she cut off his head."

Bhairav pointed through the thick foliage. "Just there. We're almost there."

"Then what?" Vikram asked, his fingers trembling slightly as he marked their GPS location.

"She didn't stop," Bhairav continued. "She escaped through the back door, locking it behind her. Then she set the house ablaze, burning everything—the bodies, the secrets, the *mantrik's* work. She emerged from the jungle, naked, holding Jaipal's severed head in one hand and burning torch in the other. She cursed the villagers, saying anyone who crossed her path would be doomed. Then she walked into the jungle, setting the sacred plant ablaze."

They pushed through a patch of dense bushes, the undergrowth clawing at their legs, until they emerged into a small clearing. In the center stood a towering ten foot statue carved from black stone. Time had not been kind to it. Crawlers and thick moss clung to its surface, while patches of fungus crept along its base. Ants marched in steady lines up its legs, and small spiders had spun delicate webs in its crevices, making it their home.

Despite the years of neglect, the statue retained an eerie presence. It depicted a woman of striking beauty and undeniable strength. Her posture was commanding, her form gracefully sculpted, even under the grime of decay. In one hand, she held a severed head, the detail so lifelike that Vikram felt a chill. Her other hand was raised in a stark, forbidding gesture—a warning to all who dared to pass.

The air around them seemed to change, the usual hum of the jungle growing quieter until it fell into an unsettling silence. Even the rustling leaves and distant birdcalls seemed to hold their breath in reverence—or fear.

"There she is, her memory in stones created by the king himself!" Bhairav said, his voice hushed. He fell to his knees and began chanting a prayer. Baburao dropped beside him and gestured for Vikram to do the same.

Vikram stared at the statue, its eerie details almost lifelike. Slowly, he knelt, bowing his head as Bhairav whispered sacred mantras. After a few minutes, Bhairav scooped a handful of earth from the base of the statue.

"All she destroyed lies behind her," Bhairav said as he stood. "The fire stopped here, and the mysteries remain buried beyond."

"But the visions, the hallucinations…" Vikram pressed.

"If the answers you seek are there, they're beyond this point," Bhairav said firmly. "No one knows how far. No one dares to go past her. This is where we stop."

"No," Vikram said, shaking his head. "If you won't come with me, I'll go alone."

Baburao grabbed his arm. "You won't. I won't allow it. Even if you go, you don't know the way or what you're looking for."

"But we have to find the truth," Vikram protested. "We have to know why people are seeing ghosts!"

"Then we ask for her permission," Bhairav said, his voice low and reverent.

Vikram hated being back at Bhairav's house. The air inside was thick with the cloying scent of burnt oil and earth, pressing down like an invisible weight. Shadows from the flickering candles stretched and twisted across the walls, and the oppressive silence felt alive, like something lurking just beyond sight. Yet he stayed, as if tethered by a strange inertia. The jungle was dangerous at night, but staying here felt like stepping into something equally perilous.

In the center of the room, Bhairav's ritual setup dominated the space. A pentagon enclosed in a circle was scrawled on the floor in crude, chalky lines. Each edge of the pentagon bore cryptic symbols—worn yet purposeful, as if they'd been passed down through generations. Five candles burned steadily at the points, their flames casting faint, trembling halos. The air was heavy with the sharp tang of scorched herbs, mingling with the metallic scent of something ancient and decayed.

Savitri sat in the center of the pentagon, her body rigid, holding a clay pot filled with mud from Chendkai's site. Her damp sari clung to her skin, revealing the sculpted contours of her shoulders, the curve of her back, and the hollow of her navel. Droplets of water glistened on her collarbone and slid down her arms, catching the flickering light. Her face, streaked with red and white paint, was a mask—beautiful, unreadable, and faintly menacing. Her wet hair dripped onto her back in uneven strands, like ink pooling on parchment.

Vikram watched her, unease prickling at the edges of his thoughts. He had been curious at first, even fascinated by the ritual's arcane symbols and strange preparations. But now, sitting here, he questioned his own motives. The air felt too thick, the fire too bright, and the quiet too loud. His gaze flicked to the clay pot in Savitri's lap. Mud. That's all it was. Mud from an old jungle. Could something so mundane truly hold power?

Beside him, Baburao sat with the calm detachment of someone who had seen this all before. His expression betrayed no shock, no hesitation. He had grown up with rituals like these, with their chants, their sacrifices, and their inevitable pain. His eyes flicked once to Savitri, lingering briefly on the tension in her arms, the faint quiver in her shoulders. There was empathy there, but it was buried beneath a lifetime of knowing that pain had always been part of belief.

Bhairav's chants began, low and guttural, each syllable dragging like a stone against the silence. He threw oil into the fire, and it flared, bathing the room in a harsh, flickering glow. The shadows on the walls danced like restless spirits, their shapes twisting into grotesque forms that seemed too real.

Vikram's eyes traced the intricate symbols carved into the floor, the five-pointed star enclosed within a circle. *Not a pentagon, a pentagram,* he corrected internally, recalling the old grimoires he had pored over—*The Key of Solomon, The Grand Grimoire, The Ars Goetia.* Protective, binding, a ward against malevolent forces. But it wasn't just the shape that unsettled him—it was the crude, almost frantic way it had been drawn, as if hastily sketched to hold something in check.

"Why the pentagram?" he whispered to Baburao, breaking the heavy silence.

"To contain her," Baburao replied, his gaze fixed on the circle. "If the lines break, we're the ones who need to worry."

Vikram frowned. *Contain her?* The implications churned in his mind. He had read of such rituals—binding rites, summoning circles, the delicate balance between control and catastrophe. *A broken seal invites chaos,* one text had warned. His questions grew heavier, but before he could voice them, Bhairav stepped forward with a whip in his hand.

Crack!

The first lash struck Savitri's back, and her body flinched violently. The clay pot wobbled in her lap but stayed upright.

Crack! Crack!

The second and third strikes tore through the damp fabric of her sari, leaving angry red welts on her skin. She didn't cry out, but her breath hitched, sharp and shallow.

"Accept her! Accept her, Savitri!" Bhairav roared, his voice shaking with fervor.

Vikram winced, his hands curling into fists. The violence clawed at him, each crack of the whip sending a jolt through his spine. He had read extensively about occult practices—theories of summoning, the necessity of ritual pain, the concept of sacrifices appeasing spirits. But reading was one thing. Watching it unfold before him was another. Especially when the victim was a woman.

His reasoning mind exploded with protest. *This is madness! Superstition!* He had always sought logic, a rational explanation behind the supernatural. Yet here he was, witnessing something straight out of the forbidden texts he had once considered academic curiosities. He wanted to look away, to stop it, but his feet remained rooted to the ground, trapped between disbelief and grim fascination.

When he turned to Baburao, expecting some flicker of hesitation, some sign of protest, he found only stillness. Baburao's gaze remained fixed on the pentagram, as though he were watching the rising flames instead of the woman in the center.

Vikram gritted his teeth. He knew, deep down, that ancient rituals often demanded blood, that spirits—if they were real—fed on sacrifice. But no amount of reading had prepared him for this.

"This is madness," Vikram muttered, his voice trembling with anger.

"It's necessary," Baburao said quietly. "The spirits demand pain. It's the only language they understand."

Vikram turned back to Savitri, but instead of her face, he saw another. His brother's. For a fleeting moment, the flames cast the ghost of his brother's features onto her contorted face—a brother he couldn't save. The memory rose like bile, bitter and accusing. The whip cracked again, and the vision vanished, leaving only guilt in its wake.

"Chendkai!" Bhairav screamed, throwing more oil into the fire. The flames surged, roaring with an intensity that felt alive. "Come, Mother! I call for you!"

Savitri's body convulsed, her head jerking back as a guttural scream tore from her throat. "Aahhhhh! Who called me? WHO?" Her voice was deep, ancient, and filled with malice. Her eyes rolled back, leaving only the whites, and her mouth foamed like a rabid animal's.

Bhairav dropped to his knees, pressing his forehead to the ground. "Chendkai! Amma… Mother!" he cried.

Savitri—or whatever now possessed her—rose to her feet. Her movements were unnatural, jerky, as if her body were being manipulated by unseen strings. She moved to the edge of the pentagon but stopped abruptly, her foot hovering just above the line. Something held her back. She began pacing, her bare feet tracing the boundary like a predator stalking its prey.

"What do you want, fool?" she spat, her voice sharp as broken glass.

"Permission, Mother!" Bhairav pleaded, his head still bowed. "We must go to the other side. We ask for your blessing!"

"FOOLS!" she roared, her voice reverberating through the room like thunder. She grabbed the pot of mud and hurled it at Bhairav. He deflected it with his arm, but the shards scattered across the floor, some slicing into his skin.

She prowled the pentagon, her fury radiating like heat from a furnace. "Have you forgotten my curse? If a single soul crosses me, I will doom you all! ALL OF YOU!" she screamed before collapsing, her body crumpling to the floor in a heap.

The fire dimmed, the oppressive heat lifting slightly. Bhairav raised his head slowly, his face pale and drenched in sweat. Savitri lay motionless, her breathing shallow. The paint on her face had streaked, mixing with tears and sweat, smearing into something twisted.

"What… what just happened?" Vikram asked, his voice a fragile whisper.

"She answered," Bhairav said hoarsely. "And the answer is no."

The ride to the bus stand was silent, the hum of Baburao's moped the only sound breaking the oppressive stillness. Vikram sat on the pillion seat, his thoughts racing as the cool night air brushed past him. The full moon hung low in the sky, its pale, indifferent light spilling over the jagged tree line, casting long shadows that seemed alive with movement.

"It's a full moon tonight," Vikram muttered under his breath, more to himself than to Baburao. "We can follow the ghost. That's all we need to do."

Baburao didn't respond, his shoulders stiff, his face set like stone. The moped bumped along the dirt path, and the jungle on either side seemed to press closer, its unseen presence heavy in the air. When they reached the bus stand, Baburao killed the engine and dismounted.

He turned to Vikram, his expression dark. "Nobody disobeys Chendkai. If she says no, we don't go. That's the end of it."

Vikram swung his leg off the moped, frustration boiling over. "You can't seriously believe this nonsense," he snapped, his voice sharp and accusing. "You're a forest officer! You—of all people—should know better!"

Baburao's eyes locked onto his, unflinching and cold. "You don't understand this jungle. You think science can explain everything. But this place isn't yours to understand—it belongs to her. Go home, Vikram. And don't ever come back."

Before Vikram could respond, Baburao turned and drove towards the shadowy village road without another word, leaving Vikram to wrestle with his own thoughts.

He boarded the waiting bus, his anger simmering just beneath the surface. The vehicle groaned to life, its headlights slicing through the darkness as it pulled away. Vikram slumped into a seat by the window, muttering to himself, "It's a full moon… it's a full moon…"

The words echoed in his mind like a mantra, growing louder, more insistent. His fingers tightened around the recorder strapped to his chest. The jungle wasn't just a place—it was calling to him, pulling him back into its shadowy embrace.

Suddenly, Vikram shot to his feet. "Stop the bus! Stop!" he yelled, his voice carrying above the engine's low rumble.

The driver cursed under his breath but brought the bus to a screeching halt. Vikram stumbled to the door, muttering a hasty excuse. "I… I forgot my wallet," he said, not meeting the driver's skeptical glare.

The bus door hissed open, and Vikram stepped into the cool night air. As the bus roared back to life and disappeared down the road, silence engulfed him. The jungle loomed ahead, a wall of black shadows and shifting leaves bathed in the pale, ethereal glow of the full moon.

He stood still for a moment, his breathing uneven. The cold light of the moon seemed to illuminate his path, as if daring him to take the first step.

And he did.

With every stride, the whispers of the jungle grew louder, tugging at the edges of his mind. The forest didn't just loom— it seemed to watch, to wait. The undergrowth rustled, the faint sound of unseen movement blending with the rustle of leaves.

Vikram's heart pounded as he walked toward the darkness, the full moon casting its cold, indifferent light over him. Somewhere in the depths of the jungle, the truth waited—but so did something far more dangerous.

He didn't stop. He didn't look back.

The Cop

*"What you perceive depends not only on what you look at,
but also, on where you're standing."*

– C.S. Lewis

The one Bed room flat was a chaotic blend of fandom and fascination. Posters of *Terminator*, *Alien*, and *Predator* fought for space on the walls with framed portraits of Darwin and Einstein, their watchful eyes adding a veneer of intellectual gravity to the otherwise messy room. A desk groaned under the weight of science books, criminal psychology manuals, and an ancient desktop computer that flickered like it was clinging to life.

On top of the TV, another larger Ganapati idol sat adorned with fresh marigold garlands. The TV barked out updates on AFR terrorist attacks while a karaoke version of *"Duniya mein, logo ko…"* blared from his phone, blending the sacred and the absurd in the air.

In the middle of it all, Siddhartha Yadav—Sid to his friends—stood in front of a mirror, performing a karaoke rendition of *"Duniya mein, logo ko…"* with the gusto of a seasoned stage performer. His khaki police uniform hung loosely on his wiry frame, but he wore it with the swagger of a Bollywood hero. As the song reached its crescendo, he slid on a pair of black sunglasses, striking a pose that could have belonged on a movie poster.

With a dramatic flair, he spun his service pistol twice on his index finger before holstering it with a satisfying click. The energy in the room was pure Sid: chaotic, over-the-top, and unapologetically entertaining.

His phone buzzed mid-performance. The name *"Chutiya Irfan"* flashed on the screen, making him chuckle as he picked it up.

"What?" Sid barked, still half-singing.

"Sir, I'm outside," came Irfan's resigned voice, muffled by the background hum of the street.

"Okay… *birraaa birraaa, tara tara tara!...* Two minutes!" Sid declared, his voice hitting a comically exaggerated high note. Without waiting for a reply, he tossed the phone in the pocket and grabbed his bike keys.

With one last glance in the mirror, Sid opened the door, humming and swaying to the tune as though the world were his stage. Before stepping out, he bowed to Ganapati with folded hands and gave the door a stylish kick. It clicked shut behind him with perfect precision, locking in place as if on cue.

Outside, Irfan sat waiting, his expression a mix of exasperation and amusement as Sid swaggered toward him, the song still trailing on his lips.

Siddhartha Yadav arrived at the crime scene with Hawaldar Irfan Khan trailing behind. A small, dingy shop stood under a faded signboard, its peeling letters barely readable in the harsh morning light. The air inside was thick, a nauseating mix of stale snacks and the unmistakable metallic tang of blood.

The shopkeeper's overweight body lay face down on the dusty floor. One hand clutched his neck as if in a futile attempt to stem the bleeding; the other gripped two rolls of duct tape. A pool of congealed blood had spread beneath his head, dark and sticky, seeping into the cracks of the worn tiles.

Outside, a small crowd had gathered, their murmurs buzzing like restless flies. A lone constable stood at the door, his outstretched arms more symbolic than effective at holding them back. Sid adjusted his sunglasses with a casual flick, his sharp eyes scanning the scene.

"No one saw anything?" he asked, his tone light, almost playful, but with an edge that made people answer him truthfully.

"They didn't—or they aren't saying," Irfan replied, his voice low as he gestured toward the crowd.

Sid tilted his head toward a tea stall across the street, its faded yellow awning flapping limply in the breeze. "That tea stall— what opens first, closes last?"

"Huh Tea Stall?" Irfan replied. "You think they didn't see something?" Sid smiled.

"I already checked," Irfan said quickly. "The owner said his stall was closed yesterday. Family wedding."

Sid's eyebrow arched behind his sunglasses. "A family wedding? How convenient. Maybe he's telling the truth. Or maybe he's the guy who gutted this fat fellow."

"You think so?" Irfan asked, startled.

Sid smirked. "Irfan, have you ever killed anyone?"

"Sir?" Irfan's eyes widened, unsure if it was a joke or a trap.

Sid stepped into the shop, the soles of his shoes making faint, deliberate squeaks against the tiled floor. "How will you catch a killer if you don't think like one?" he called over his shoulder.

Irfan followed hesitantly, his confusion written all over his face.

Sid crouched near the body, pointing toward the duct tape and rope stacked on the counter. "Here's how it went: I walk into this shop, ask for duct tape and rope. I hand over four hundred rupees." He gestured to the crumpled notes tucked under the register. "More than enough for just these two things, don't you think?"

Irfan nodded slowly, starting to see where Sid was going.

"I paid, 400 rupees! I didn't come in here planning to kill," Sid continued, his voice steady, almost conversational. "But then something happens. Maybe he sees something he shouldn't. Maybe he says something he shouldn't."

Sid mimed a quick, clean stabbing motion toward his neck. "And then? Bam. Right in the jugular."

Irfan leaned closer, his eyes widening. "The wound matches the direction of the attack!"

"Exactly," Sid said, straightening up and brushing off imaginary dust from his khakis. "Now, the real question: was it premeditated, or did this escalate? Definitely escalation!"

Before Irfan could respond, Sid turned on his heel and walked out of the shop, his voice carrying back over his shoulder. "Let's get some tea. A good murder always deserves a good chai."

At the tea stall, Sid sipped his tea, holding the steaming cup lightly in his hands as he surveyed the surroundings with an air of practiced ease. Nearby, Irfan leaned over the counter, questioning the vendor.

"So, you closed early yesterday for a wedding?" Irfan asked, his tone casual but probing.

"Yes, Sir. By noon," the vendor replied, wiping his hands on a stained towel. "Had to leave for the next village. Didn't reopen until this morning."

Sid glanced at the vendor over the rim of his cup. "You needed duct tape and rope?" he asked lightly, his voice carrying just enough curiosity to make the man pause.

The vendor blinked in confusion. "What? No, Sir! Why would I need duct tape and rope?"

Sid's lips curled into a smirk as he set his tea down. "Exactly. Why would a tea vendor need duct tape and rope?" He let the question hang in the air, raising an eyebrow toward Irfan. Irfan frowned, clearly trying to piece together whether Sid was hinting at something deeper or just being cryptic.

Before Irfan could respond, Sid's phone buzzed in his pocket. He answered with his usual nonchalance.

"Sid, where are you?" came the inspector's gruff voice on the other end.

"At the scene, Sir. Waiting for forensics," Sid replied breezily.

"Forget that for now," the inspector ordered. "There's another murder about thirty kilometers from your location. Locals are calling it road rage. Head there and manage until the team arrives."

"Yes, Sir," Sid said, ending the call without hesitation.

Tossing a few bills onto the counter, he turned to the constable guarding the shop. "Kiran, hold things here until forensics shows up. We've got an invitation ahead!"

The constable nodded in affirmation, and before Irfan could process the abrupt shift, Sid had already mounted his Bajaj Pulsar. He revved the engine with the flourish of a man born to be dramatic.

"Chal, Irfan! Adventure awaits!" Sid called out, patting the seat behind him with mock impatience.

Irfan climbed on, muttering something under his breath about reckless bosses. As Sid kicked the stand and started the bike, he burst into song, his voice ringing out over the rumble of the engine:

"Jadu teri nazar… khushboo… tu hai meri Kiran…"

The bike roared to life, speeding down the dusty road. A cloud of dust swirled in their wake, leaving the tea stall vendor shaking his head in bemusement.

At the second scene, Sid knelt beside a body sprawled near a fallen Vespa. Blood stained the man's jeans, and his neck bore dark rope burns, stark against his pale skin. The moped lay a few meters away, its left mirror shattered and streaks of blood smearing the ground nearby.

"Strangulation," Sid muttered, carefully tilting the man's head for a closer look. "Most likely with a rope."

Irfan crouched near the Vespa, his brow furrowed. "Doesn't look like anyone hit it."

"No collision," Sid agreed, his gaze sweeping the ground. He gestured to the scratches and blood trail. "He fell. Left side mirror's broken—scratches match the skid. He must've pulled his leg free in a hurry and bled from the scrape."

Irfan tilted his head. "But why would he run?"

"Why, indeed?" Sid murmured, his eyes narrowing as he surveyed the scene.

With a sudden burst of energy, Sid began retracing the victim's presumed movements. He jogged a few steps, exaggerated a fall, and rolled onto his side, mimicking the victim's escape. With theatrical flair, he dragged one leg free and limped toward the body's final position.

Nearby, a few women standing by the road giggled at the performance, their hands covering their mouths. A group of younger girls watched with wide eyes, their expressions caught between amusement and curiosity. One of them smiled shyly at Sid, who flashed a grin and tipped his sunglasses in response.

Irfan, struggling to keep a straight face, crossed his arms. "What did you find, Sherlock?"

"Nothing," Sid admitted with a shrug, his grin widening. He adjusted his uniform and glanced back at the smiling girl. "But it was fun, wasn't it?"

The younger constable shook his head, muttering under his breath, "This guy's something else."

Sid turned serious, his grin fading. "Alright, back to work. Let's figure out what scared him enough to run like that." He scanned the surroundings again, his sharp eyes searching for clues. The women, meanwhile, whispered among themselves, their giggles trailing off as Sid's attention refocused on the investigation.

Sid stood in front of a large map of Maharashtra and Karnataka pinned to the wall, its surface dotted with red pins marking various locations. Nearby, Irfan sat on a creaky chair, watching as Sid pressed another pin into place.

"We got a missing person report, didn't we?" Sid asked, not taking his eyes off the board.

"Yes, Sir. A girl traveling from Kolhapur to Goa. Her last call was made from here." Irfan handed him a note. Sid glanced at it and pushed another pin directly over an already-marked location.

"And wasn't a stolen scooter found at the same spot?" Sid murmured, his tone more of a statement than a question.

"Yes," Irfan said, his voice tinged with realization.

Before either could say more, Inspector Sanjay Mali entered the room. Irfan shot to his feet, saluting sharply. Sid, as usual, didn't bother with formalities, and Sanjay didn't seem to care.

"How's your daughter, Irfan? Fifth standard, right?" Sanjay asked conversationally, glancing at the board.

"She's doing well, Sir. Yes, in fifth," Irfan replied, his chest puffing slightly with pride.

"They grow up too fast," Sanjay said with a brief smile before turning his attention to Sid. "And you? When's the wedding?"

"June, Sir," Sid replied, his focus still on the map.

Sid was born into a family that believed in duty, honor, and discipline. His father was a decorated police officer, a man who never bent the rules, never let his emotions interfere. Sid was nothing like him. He grew up questioning authority, bending rules when necessary, and believing that justice wasn't always written in ink, but sometimes in blood. His mother, a loving and caring woman, died when he was in college.

The shock was immense, but Sid did what he always did— turned grief into fuel, pain into punchlines. He accepted the world for what it was and laughed his way through it. It made him the most stylish, loved, and effortlessly magnetic guy on campus.

That's when Kavita happened. A girl just a year junior to him, smart, headstrong, and with zero patience for bullshit— which made it all the more ironic that she fell for the biggest bullshitter on campus.

The incident was simple. It involved a stray dog, an ice cream cone, and an unfortunate misunderstanding that nearly got Sid arrested.

It started when Sid was walking across campus, licking a melting ice cream cone, minding his own business.

Enter Sheru—a huge, overenthusiastic stray dog that had somehow decided Sid was his one true love.

Sheru came barreling down the pathway like a missile, tongue out, tail wagging like a possessed windshield wiper. Sid barely had time to react before the dog leaped—directly at his chest.

Sid stumbled backward, flailing, the ice cream flying straight into Kavita's hands.

She had been walking toward the library, completely oblivious, when suddenly—bam. A half-melted scoop of chocolate **splat** right in her palms.

She froze. Sid froze. Sheru proudly wagged his tail.

Before anyone could process what had just happened, a security guard sprinted onto the scene, pointing a baton at Sid.

"YOU!" the guard barked. "What did you just THROW at her!?"

Sid blinked, still holding his now-empty cone.

"Uh. Ice cream?"

The security guard did not look convinced. "Miss, are you okay? Do you want to file a complaint?"

Kavita, still holding the melting mess in her hands, took a slow, measured breath.

Then, she smeared it across Sid's face.

"Yes," she said. "I'd like to file a complaint… about his terrible taste in flavors."

Three years later, they were finally getting married.

Sid stood with marker in his hands, when Sanjay let out a sigh.

"June, right? I forgot." He rubbed his temples, exhaustion creeping into his voice. "The commissioner's office was a nightmare today."

Sid smirked. "What happened? Did they finally declare you unfit for duty?"

"Delhi Police," Sanjay grumbled, ignoring him. "They've started wearing masks now, like the central forces. The commissioner thinks we should follow their example."

Sid's smirk faded.

"Masks? What, like ski masks? Gas masks? Superhero masks?"

Sanjay shot him a look. "Anti-pollution masks, idiot. You know, because we're all apparently breathing poison now."

Sid exhaled through his nose, tapping his fingers on the armrest. "Criminals wear masks because they want to hide their identity." He looked at Sanjay. "Who the hell are the police hiding from?"

Sanjay hesitated, then muttered, "Cameras, journalists… maybe hiding from their true responsibility."

"So this is what the world is coming to?" Sid let out a slow breath, shaking his head.

"For now, it's pending. Let's pray it stays that way," Sanjay said, shaking his head. "Anyway, where are we on the missing girl case? There's pressure from above—her family has connections."

Sid gestured at the map. "This is where she made her last call—to her boyfriend. She mentioned a flat tire." He pointed to another pin. "And this is where we found a stolen scooter abandoned."

"And these other pins?" Sanjay asked, leaning closer.

"This one marks the shopkeeper's murder—where rope and duct tape were stolen. And here, we found a Vespa rider strangled to death," Sid explained.

Irfan's eyes widened. "You think it's all connected?"

"It's obvious," Sid replied. "Two guys steal a scooter, find a stranded girl, and either lure her in or kidnap her. They abandon the scooter, take her car, and stop for supplies. The shopkeeper gets suspicious, so they kill him."

"And the Vespa rider?" Irfan asked.

"They couldn't risk him reporting what he saw," Sid said. "He's collateral damage."

Sanjay nodded thoughtfully. "So, what's the next step?"

Sid traced a route on the map with his finger. "This road leads to the Goa highway. But there's another path here—a secluded one that branches into the jungle."

"Unlikely they'd head to Goa with a girl in the trunk," Irfan said.

"Exactly. I'll take the remote road and ask around. Irfan, you take the highway," Sid instructed.

Sanjay sighed. "We're short on manpower. These rebels are a nightmare, and now this case."

Sid flashed his signature grin. "We don't need an army, Sir. Just a good plan."

Sanjay chuckled dryly. "Fine. Get me something solid to work with."

As he turned to leave, Sid spun his colt theatrically. "Sir, one request."

"What now?" Sanjay asked, half-smiling.

"Bullets," Sid said, holding up the empty weapon.

Sanjay pulled out his Glock, ejecting the magazine to reveal just three bullets. "You're lucky you even have a gun," he said, reloading it. "Point it. Most people behave without you having to shoot."

Sid watched him leave, then turned to the board. With a dramatic flourish, he snapped his colt shut and called out, "Muzak!"

A lady constable hit play on the boombox, and the room filled with the beats of *Jaan Pehchaan Ho*. Sid spun on his heels, breaking into an exaggerated dance, his hips swaying to the rhythm.

"Show-off," Irfan muttered, smiling despite himself.

The Pursuit

"The journey not the arrival matters."

– T.S. Eliot

Maya held her phone close to her ear, her voice trembling slightly. "Nasreen, I had to leave in a hurry… Yes, I'm going to look for him there. I don't know, but maybe he came back. He… he wanted to know the truth." She paused, lowering her voice. "Don't worry, I'll be careful. I'll see you once I'm back… Dinner? Yeah, sure." She hesitated, the words catching in her throat. "I wanted to tell you something… I think—" The signal buzzed, cutting her off.

She let out a frustrated sigh, staring at the blank screen. *Love you*, she thought, biting her lip. *Maybe next time, I should just kiss her.* It was her first time thinking of proposing to someone, and she couldn't shake the sense of missed timing. *Proposing over the phone is wrong anyway*, she told herself, trying to turn her disappointment into something positive. *It's good the signal dropped. Some things are meant to be said in person.*

The bus rattled forward on a desolate road, the engine groaning with every bump. Outside, the landscape blurred into a monotonous stretch of dry fields and gnarled trees. The driver sat silent, his face a mask of focus, navigating the route as though he could do it blindfolded. Maya was the only passenger, her bag pressed against her chest like a shield.

The conductor, a middle-aged man with a weathered face and a voice steeped in village inflections, shuffled toward her. "Dongarwadi is about a half-hour walk from the last stop," he said. "Who're you going to meet there? I've got relatives in the area, so I'm curious."

"Baburao," Maya replied simply.

"Baburao? Babya Kamble?" His tone shifted slightly, his eyebrows lifting in recognition. Maya nodded.

"Ah, that guy! He's a friend of mine. So... you're his?" The man's curiosity was laced with a teasing edge.

"Nobody," Maya said firmly, brushing off the implication. "I just need help with the jungle. He's the one to ask, right?"

The conductor chuckled. "He sure is. Baburao's the only person who can step into that jungle and come back with his sanity intact. Quite the celebrity around here."

"What do you mean, 'the only person'?" Maya asked, her curiosity piqued.

The conductor's expression darkened. "That jungle... it's cursed. Haunted. Take my advice, kid—stay away."

"Haunted?" Maya pressed, leaning forward.

"Ghosts," the conductor muttered, glancing nervously out the window. "People say they see their dead relatives calling to them from the woods. Others believe there's some kind of... passage to another world in there." His voice dropped lower, his eyes darting to the rising line of trees on the horizon.

"Have you ever seen anything?" Maya asked.

"Thankfully, no," he said, shaking his head. "But that driver up there—" he gestured toward the man behind the wheel, whose face remained stoic—"he had a scare once. Didn't leave his house for a week afterward."

"What happened?" Maya leaned in, her voice tinged with anticipation.

The conductor lowered his voice to a conspiratorial whisper. "It was a full moon. We were late, running this same route.

The driver parked near the jungle to take a leak, thinking the stories were just that—stories. I stayed on the bus, scared stiff. A few minutes later, he comes running back, pale as a ghost. Wouldn't stop driving until we were miles away. He's never told me what he saw, but whatever it was… it shook him."

"And yet he still drives this route?" Maya asked, glancing at the stoic driver.

The conductor shrugged. "Some people are strange like that. But Baburao… he's different. He walks the jungle even on full-moon nights. Funny thing is, back in college, he wasn't brave at all. Timid, actually. Got bullied a lot. Then one day…"

The conductor hesitated, his voice trailing off.

"What happened?" Maya prompted.

"They found a tumor in his brain," the conductor said after a pause. "He needed surgery. Changed him. Became a little… slow, you know? Crazy, some might say. He lost a year and a half, but he came back stronger. Finished college. Became the man he is now."

Maya nodded. "Sounds like a real fighter."

The conductor leaned closer, his expression serious. "Kid, take my advice—drop this idea of going into that jungle. It's not a place for people like you."

Before Maya could respond, the bus screeched to a halt at the edge of the village. The conductor stepped off, pointing toward a lonely dirt road. "Walk another five kilometers, and you'll reach Dongarwadi," he said, his tone carrying both concern and challenge. "Or… turn back now."

Maya tightened her grip on her bag and stepped off the bus, her feet crunching against the dry earth. As the vehicle rumbled away, she stood alone, the forest looming ahead like a dark, waiting sentinel.

What have I gotten myself into? she thought, taking her first step down the deserted path toward Dongarwadi.

Maya had been walking for about half a kilometer when the faint hum of a moped reached her ears. She turned, spotting two men emerging from a narrow pathway that cut through the trees. The moped wobbled slightly as it merged onto the main road, carrying two middle-aged men.

The moped passed her but braked abruptly just ahead. Maya kept walking, her gaze fixed on the men as they turned to look at her.

"Hey, kid! Where are you headed?" one of them called out, his voice gruff but curious.

She stopped a few paces from them. "Dongarwadi," she replied firmly.

"Dongarwadi? What for?" The man who spoke climbed off the moped, scrutinizing her with sharp, weathered eyes. His presence exuded authority, though his worn clothes and the mud-streaked moped suggested a simple life.

"I'm looking for the forest guide... Baburao," she said, studying his reaction.

The man exchanged a glance with his companion, a wiry fellow with darting eyes. The first man let out a short laugh, though his expression remained serious.

"Baburao?" he repeated, then turned off the moped's engine. "That's me."

Maya's heart skipped. The coincidence felt surreal, almost too perfect. She straightened her shoulders, relieved but cautious, and explained her purpose, detailing her connection to Vikram and the circumstances of his disappearance.

Baburao listened intently, his dark eyes unwavering. The wiry man—Bhairav—folded his arms and frowned, muttering under his breath.

"So, he hasn't returned?" Baburao asked, his voice measured but concerned.

"No," Maya said, her tone steady. "It's been six months. I suspect he came back here."

Baburao scratched his chin thoughtfully, glancing at Bhairav. "He was here," Baburao admitted. "But we put him on the bus."

"That bastard!" Bhairav snapped, throwing his hands in the air. "He must've gotten off and gone back into the jungle!"

"This is not good. This is not good," Bhairav added, his voice rising with a mix of fear and frustration.

Baburao shot him a sharp look. "Get a grip. We don't know that for sure."

Bhairav shook his head, his face pale. "If he crossed the Goddess... Foolish man. He doesn't know what he's done."

"What goddess?" Maya asked, trying to piece together the cryptic exchange.

Baburao's eyes locked on hers, his expression unreadable. He hesitated for a moment before turning and climbing back onto the moped. He started the engine, the low rumble breaking the tense silence.

"Hop on," he said, his tone brisk.

There was hardly any space, but Bhairav was a thin man.

"Don't worry, there's room," Baburao said dryly. "I'll explain on the way."

She hesitated for a moment but then climbed on, squeezing into the tight space behind Bhairav. Her body pressed against his thin frame, and she caught the faint, musky scent of sweat lingering on his skin. The moped lurched forward, its engine coughing as they set off toward Dongarwadi.

The forest loomed closer, its dense canopy casting shadows over the road as Maya clung to the edge of the seat. The wind carried the faint scent of earth and damp leaves, but beneath it lingered something sharper, almost metallic—a smell she couldn't quite place. Baburao began explaining, his voice raised to cut through the rush of air. The trees seemed to lean closer as though listening to every word.

The Encounter

– Friedrich Nietzsche

Sid stood at the bifurcation, his gaze shifting between the two paths. To the right, the tarred road stretched smoothly into the distance. To the left, a muddy trail wound its way deeper into the jungle, flanked by towering trees that clawed at the darkening sky. He switched off his bike's engine and walked toward the muddy path, crouching to inspect the ground.

Tire marks. A car had been through here recently.

He straightened, his eyes scanning the surroundings. A weathered wooden signboard stood nearby, with *Khandav* crudely painted on it. A red cross had been hastily drawn over the name, as if warning travelers to turn back. The paintwork looked childish, almost mocking.

The forest around him was eerily still. The occasional hoot of a distant monkey broke the silence, but it only added to the unease. The canopy above was so dense that the setting sun was hidden, though the orange hues of the sky bled through in patches. He judged he had maybe an hour before darkness consumed the jungle entirely.

Sid checked his phone. No signal. At least the battery was full.

Should I wait until morning? The thought lingered briefly before he pushed it aside. Every minute lost was another moment Swati might suffer—if she was still alive. Gritting his teeth, he climbed back onto his bike and followed the muddy trail, his eyes tracing the tire marks ahead.

After two or three kilometers, he spotted it—a red Verna parked haphazardly at the side of the road. His breath hitched as he noticed a figure sprawled across the car's roof.

Sid slowed to a stop, parking his bike behind the car. The jungle around him felt oppressive, the shadows deepening with every passing moment. He approached cautiously, scanning the area for any sign of movement. Nothing. Only the trees, their skeletal branches twisting like frozen specters against the dimming light.

He climbed onto the car's roof to get a closer look. The body was that of a man—Manoj. His lifeless face stared up at the sky, neck torn apart in a brutal attack. Dried, dark blood streaked across the windshield below, a monstrous testament to the violence that had unfolded.

Sid's gaze shifted to Manoj's right hand, which still gripped a *desi katta*. He squatted beside the body, his mind racing. Something must have attacked him—an animal, maybe a leopard? He looked up into the tangled canopy above but saw no signs of claw marks on the body.

Frowning, Sid examined the katta. The single-shot firearm was empty. He guessed it had already been fired in desperation. Checking Manoj's pockets, he found five 9mm rounds.

He grinned faintly, pulling out his Glock 17. "Just point, no need to shoot. Easy enough, right? Tell that to the animals," he muttered under his breath, loading the rounds into his empty magazine.

Sid stood on the car's roof, his gun raised, scanning his surroundings like a man preparing for a final clash. He pointed the weapon in all directions, muttering under his breath, "Come on, you motherfucker." His eyes darted upward, and he aimed at the branches above. "*Hmm… something jumped from up there!*" he murmured.

Dropping his gaze to the scene below, he stepped off the roof and crouched near the hood. His eyes caught the trail of blood—faint smears leading to handprints that seemed to crawl toward the car's front. He followed the marks, his brow furrowed.

"The girl. It must be the girl. It carried her… whatever it was," he muttered, his voice tinged with unease. The knife lay discarded on the ground, dulled and bloodstained, next to the frayed ropes.

Sid knelt closer, inspecting the handprints in the dirt. They looked human… but something was wrong. The proportions were all off. The fingers were grotesquely long, the ratios unnatural. His stomach churned as he traced the markings with his eyes. The nails—thick, jagged, and claw-like—had left deep scratches on the car's hood, their edges curling slightly as if they belonged to no human or animal he'd ever seen.

"Animal. Clearly an animal," he said to himself, trying to convince his racing mind. But doubt lingered. This wasn't just any animal—it was something else. Something different. Something wrong. The light was fading fast now. Shadows lengthened and crept toward Sid as the forest seemed to come alive with the rustle of leaves and distant, indistinct noises. He felt the weight of the growing darkness, an almost tangible presence in the air.

He remained there, knife in hand, as if waiting for the jungle itself to make its next move.

Sid stood motionless for a long time, his eyes scanning the ground, trying to make sense of the scene. The spot where Dilip had been killed was marked only by a dark, dried stain of blood on the stone. The body was gone. The disturbed mud nearby told a grim story—something, or someone, had dragged it away.

He crouched and examined the footprints scattered in the dirt. Most were ordinary, left by boots or sneakers, but one set was strange. The prints were incomplete, misshapen, and they vanished abruptly into the thick jungle.

So the boys jacked the car with the girl and came here for... obvious reasons. But something attacked them, he thought. His gaze shifted to the red Verna parked ahead, where Manoj's body lay sprawled across the roof. *One of the boys is dead. But where are the others? And what happened to the girl?*

As the sun dipped below the horizon, the jungle began to change. The tall trees, their branches reaching upward like gnarled claws, turned into looming black silhouettes. The hum of crickets filled the air, their sharp, rhythmic calls unnerving in the silence. The occasional howl of wolves punctuated the darkness, a chilling reminder of how far he was from safety.

Sid shivered, brushing his fingers across the Glock at his side. *Damn it. I can't go back to the station for backup; everyone's busy with the riots in the city. Maybe I should stay in a nearby village for the night and return in the morning with a search party.*

Resolving to leave, he climbed onto his bike and turned the ignition. The headlight pierced through the dense shadows, casting fleeting glimpses of the trail ahead. He began to turn the bike around, the beam cutting through the trees and the oppressive darkness of the jungle.

Then, he heard it.

"Sid."

The voice was faint, barely audible over the growl of the engine. He froze, his hands gripping the handlebars tightly.

"Sid, over here," it came again, louder this time, tinged with desperation.

He killed the engine. Silence enveloped him as he listened, his breath shallow.

"Over here!"

The words were clear now. They came from the shadows, and his heart thudded painfully in his chest. He turned toward the sound, his eyes straining in the dim light.

Her form wavered, ghostlike, as she stepped closer. Her dress was torn in several places, her hair tangled and disheveled. Barefoot and staggering, she seemed on the verge of collapse. But as the light from his headlamp caught her face, a jolt of recognition surged through him.

It was unmistakably her—the girl from the photographs he had studied endlessly. Every detail of her face matched perfectly: the delicate curve of her jaw, the slight dimple in her chin, the soft arch of her brows.

Sid's initial relief was quickly swallowed by unease. *How does she know my name?*

"Are you okay? Can you walk?" he called out, his voice steady but cautious.

Swati stopped and looked up at him. A faint smile touched her lips, serene and unsettling. "Now that you're here, I feel fine," she said softly, her tone unnervingly calm.

Sid frowned. *This isn't right.*

"I need your help," Swati said suddenly, her voice firm but distant. "Come with me. It's this way."

She gestured toward the jungle, her hand trembling slightly.

"This way? Deeper into the jungle?" Sid asked, his unease mounting. "I can take you to the city. You'll be safe there."

"No," she said sharply, her eyes flashing with something unnameable. "I need help… in the jungle. It's where I belong."

His instincts screamed at him to leave. But something about her voice struck him—a strange familiarity that felt almost like his own thoughts reflected back at him.

The rustling began then, faint but deliberate. It came from behind him, growing louder with each second.

"What was that?" Sid asked, his voice steady but his hand instinctively going to his Glock.

"Nothing to worry about," Swati said, her smile returning. "Just… come with me."

The air around him felt heavier, thick with an unidentifiable scent—earthy, sweet, and strangely alluring. Sid felt his pulse quicken.

His eyes darted toward the car. Manoj's body was still sprawled across the roof, but something was wrong. Slowly, impossibly, the lifeless form began to move, its limbs twitching unnaturally.

His breath caught in his throat as Manoj's head turned, blood dripping steadily from the gaping wound in his neck. His milky, lifeless eyes locked onto Sid.

"No," Sid whispered, stepping back.

Swati stepped forward, her hand brushing his arm. "Don't be afraid," she said softly. "You're safe with me. You've always been safe with me."

Sid's grip on his Glock tightened, but his feet refused to move. His mind felt clouded, his thoughts no longer his own.

"Come with me," Swati repeated, her voice echoing strangely in the dense jungle. "We have to go deeper."

Manoj slid off the car, his movements jerky and unnatural, stepping into the shadows like a puppet on strings. Sid's vision swam, the scent around him growing stronger.

His subconscious urged him forward, but his conscious mind rebelled. *This isn't real! It can't be real!*

"No," Sid whispered, his voice hoarse.

He stumbled back toward his bike, fighting the pull of the jungle and its hallucinatory whispers. "I'm leaving," he muttered, gripping the handlebars.

Manoj took a step closer, his movements growing smoother, more deliberate. Swati's voice followed, soft and inviting. "Why run, Sid? You belong here."

Sid revved the engine, the sound cutting through the oppressive silence. "Hop on, if you want to live!" he shouted, his voice trembling but firm.

Swati looked at him, then back at Manoj, her expression unreadable. After a brief pause, she moved closer and climbed onto the bike. Her hands wrapped around his torso, and he shivered. They were icy—unnaturally cold, as if they were draining the warmth from his body.

The shadows seemed to retreat momentarily as the headlight flared to life. He turned the bike sharply, accelerating down the path, the roar of the engine filling the night.

"How do you know my name?" he asked, his voice cutting through the wind.

"Why shouldn't I? We are going the wrong direction. This is not where I can go…" Swati replied, her tone worried but distant.

"What? I'm not a celebrity or something…" He turned his head slightly to look at her, but as his eyes flicked back, his heart dropped.

She wasn't there.

Her hands, or at least the sensation of them, still clung to his waist—cold and unrelenting—but the seat behind him was empty.

A chill raced down his spine. He gasped, his grip faltering as panic surged through him.

Distracted, he missed the sharp turn ahead.

The bike veered off the trail, plunging into the jungle. Branches whipped at him as the bike careened through the undergrowth, skidding before colliding with a tree.

The impact threw Sid forward. His head struck the bark with a sickening crack, and the world spun wildly.

As his vision blurred and darkness began to claim him, he saw her. Swati.

She stood over him, her torn dress swaying as if caught in a breeze. Her smile was wide now, unnatural, almost predatory. Her face blurred, shifting in and out of focus, but her eyes—those gleaming, unholy eyes—remained fixed on him.

Then, everything went black.

The Meeting

"There is no meeting of minds, no point of understanding,
but one of pure survival."

– H.P. Lovecraft

Ramu Kaka, the village head, paced furiously across the creaking wooden porch of his ancestral home, his voice echoing through the tense silence.

"You took him to Chendkai?" he bellowed, glaring at Baburao and Bhairav. "Are you out of your minds?"

Baburao shifted uncomfortably, his gaze fixed on the ground. "But we didn't cross…" he muttered faintly.

Ramu Kaka's eyes narrowed, his voice cutting like a blade. "You are unaffected, Babu. Somehow, the jungle has accepted you. But what about the others? What about the rest of us?"

He turned sharply to Bhairav, his voice rising with frustration. "And you—you should know better! What was it? Why? Did he pay you?"

Baburao and Bhairav exchanged guilty glances, then looked down. Ramu sighed in frustration, nodding to himself as if he'd expected no better.

Maya stood at the edge of the porch, her arms crossed tightly over her chest, trying to stay composed. She felt like an outsider in every sense of the word. The wary glances from the villagers, the oppressive atmosphere of the jungle, even the unnatural quiet in the air—it all pressed down on her like a weight she couldn't shake. This was nothing like the city she had grown up in. Watching Ramu, she couldn't help but feel like a scolded child witnessing a patriarch's wrath.

Finally, Ramu stopped pacing, his piercing gaze turning to her. "Six months, you say?" he asked sharply.

Maya straightened, willing her voice to stay steady. "Yes… it's been six months since he disappeared."

Six months. *How long could someone survive in a place like this?* Her chest tightened at the thought of Vikram—his sharp mind, his stubborn curiosity. She had seen him as invincible, but now… now she wasn't so sure.

Ramu's face darkened. "He definitely went back. That's why we're seeing these things so frequently. He disobeyed the Goddess." His fists clenched at his sides, his voice thick with anger—and something deeper, almost primal—fear.

"You city people," he spat, his words dripping with contempt. "You understand nothing."

The words stung more than Maya expected. Her pulse quickened, the urge to defend herself rising, but she bit her tongue. He had every right to be angry. But this wasn't her fault. Lowering her eyes, she fought to keep her emotions in check. The last thing she needed was to alienate the only people who might help her.

Ramu sighed deeply, the tension in his shoulders softening slightly. "Sorry. It's not your fault," he muttered, more to himself than to her.

The villagers remained quiet, their eyes darting between Ramu and Bhairav, waiting for direction. Moments passed in strained silence before Ramu spoke again, this time addressing Bhairav directly.

"We can ask for her forgiveness," Bhairav said faintly, his voice barely audible.

"Yes," Ramu agreed quickly. "Can we do it tomorrow?"

Bhairav nodded. "Yes… yes, we can."

Ramu pointed at one of the villagers. "Bring everything Bhairav needs first thing in the morning. We must calm the Goddess. We must ask for her forgiveness."

The villager nodded and hurried off.

Ramu turned to Baburao, his gaze intense. "But we need to find that professor. Hope he's still alive… Six months is a long time."

Maya's throat tightened. The thought of finding Vikram's body—or worse, not finding anything at all—sent a shiver through her. His mother's face flashed in her mind, the faith she had placed in Maya overwhelming her with guilt. You came here for answers. Stay focused, she told herself firmly.

Baburao scratched the back of his neck. "He's a botany professor. He knows plants. He can survive in the jungle… probably."

Ramu's expression darkened further. "Plants, yes. But ghosts? That's a different matter."

The air grew heavier as Ramu's voice dropped. "Babu, can you search for him?"

Baburao hesitated, glancing nervously at Bhairav. "Beyond the Goddess? Huh… I… I can try," he stammered.

Ramu nodded grimly. "We cannot ask for forgiveness while he's still out there. Can we?" He looked at Bhairav.

Bhairav's voice, though quiet, carried weight. "Yes. We must be certain. Without it, the ritual will fail."

"Go early morning," Ramu commanded. "And return by evening. We'll start the ceremony once you're back."

Ramu's gaze shifted to the villagers. "Does anyone volunteer to join him?"

The question hung in the air like a curse. The villagers remained mute, their faces pale and unreadable. Everyone knew Baburao was special—accepted by the jungle, spared by the spirits—but they were not.

"I will," Maya said suddenly, her voice cutting through the silence.

The words escaped before she could second-guess herself. The tension in the room shifted as every head turned to her, eyes wide with disbelief. A small, doubtful voice in the back of her mind questioned her impulsiveness, but she silenced it. This was her responsibility. She couldn't stand by while others risked their lives for her cause.

"No, no," Ramu said firmly. "We cannot allow it. The jungle isn't safe for outsiders. And you are a woman!"

"It's my job," Maya replied, her voice unwavering. "I came here to find him, and I will."

Murmurs rippled through the crowd. "Let her go," one villager called out. Then another voice echoed in agreement.

Ramu raised a hand for silence, his sharp gaze piercing through the dissent. He turned to Baburao. "Are you okay with this, Babu?"

Baburao hesitated, glancing at Maya. "Any company would help," he admitted quietly.

"So be it," Ramu declared, raising his hands in a gesture of finality.

Maya exhaled, her shoulders relaxing slightly. She could feel the villagers' eyes on her, their judgment heavy and unrelenting. Straightening her back, she met Ramu's gaze briefly before turning to Baburao.

She wouldn't let fear dictate her actions—not now, not when she was so close to the answers she'd come searching for.

The jungle awaited them, and with it, whatever answers—or horrors—it held.

Moment of Truth

"We're all mad here."

– Alice in the wonderland

Vikram moved silently through the jungle, the soft crunch of his boots blending with the rustling leaves above. The GPS in his hand glowed faintly, its dim light guiding him toward Chendkai. The full moon hung overhead, its silvery glow piercing through the dense canopy. The air was cool, carried on a gentle breeze, yet the night felt heavy, as if the jungle itself held its breath.

He spoke into his recorder, his voice steady but tinged with apprehension. "Thirty minutes in. No signs of anything unusual."

The jungle teemed with its usual noises—the hum of crickets, the occasional owl's distant call, the rustle of unseen creatures. Yet, beneath these sounds, there was a dissonance, an unsettling undercurrent that made Vikram's pulse quicken.

"Chendkai is about fifteen minutes ahead," he continued, his voice lower. "I don't know what I'll find, but…" His flashlight swept across the undergrowth, shadows jumping and twisting. "…no ghosts. It's a full moon, and… SHYAM!"

Vikram froze, his heart pounding as his flashlight's beam caught the figure ahead. It stood partially obscured by the trees, its silhouette human but unnervingly still. Shadows pooled around its feet, the moonlight doing little to illuminate its features.

"Shyam?" Vikram whispered, his voice cracking. The name escaped him instinctively, but dread immediately clamped down on his chest.

The figure didn't move.

Vikram's breath quickened, misting in the suddenly cold air. He raised the flashlight, the beam flickering as though the batteries were faltering. The light cut through the shadows, but what it revealed didn't offer relief—it only deepened his terror. The figure stepped forward, its movements eerily smooth, almost gliding through the foliage.

It was Shyam.

Or… it looked like him.

"Brother!" Shyam's voice rang out, warm and familiar, but something was wrong—there was an undercurrent to it, a layered echo that made Vikram's skin crawl. "You came back for me!"

Vikram staggered backward, his legs threatening to buckle. His mind scrambled to process what he was seeing. Shyam's face was perfect—too perfect. His features were untouched by the years that had passed, his clothes pristine, his eyes too bright in the pale light. A hint of a smile played on his lips, but it was off—like someone trying to mimic a human expression without fully understanding it.

"No… no, this isn't real," Vikram stammered, shaking his head. "You're not real. You're dead."

"Dead?" Shyam tilted his head, the movement too sharp, too precise. His smile widened unnaturally, exposing teeth that gleamed like polished ivory. "Do I look dead, brother?"

Vikram's pulse thundered in his ears. His fingers trembled as he gripped the flashlight tighter, angling it toward Shyam's feet. But there was no shadow. The ground beneath him was bare.

Shyam stepped closer, his bare feet making no sound on the forest floor. "After all this time," he said, his voice dripping with mock affection. "You still doubt me. Look at me, Vikram. Don't you recognize your own brother?"

Vikram stood frozen, disbelief and emotion washing over him in waves. Then, as if on instinct, he stepped forward and reached out, his hands hovering near Shyam's shoulders before stopping. A cold, biting sensation radiated from Shyam's form, making Vikram recoil.

"How is this possible?" Vikram murmured, his voice barely audible. "You're not Shyam."

Vikram stepped back, pulling out his GoPro with trembling fingers. He aimed it at Shyam. "I can see him through the camera!" he muttered into his recorder. "If you're watching this later, he was real. Isn't he?"

Shyam tilted his head, his lips curling into a faint smile. "Still doubting me? Even your camera agrees." He gestured to Vikram's hand, which still clutched the recorder.

"Cameras don't see," Vikram muttered. "Its mind that see's through camera!" Vikram's rationality fought for dominance. "You're… a hallucination," he said, his voice growing firmer. "You haven't aged. That's impossible."

"Maybe I'm a ghost, and ghosts don't age," Shyam replied, his tone nonchalant. "Or maybe I'm exactly what you've been searching for."

Vikram's breath hitched as he felt an invisible pull, a compulsion gnawing at the edges of his mind. His grip on the flashlight slackened, and his legs moved of their own accord, drawing him closer to the thing that wore his brother's face.

"Come with me," Shyam said softly, extending a hand. His voice had lost its warmth, replaced by a cold, commanding tone that sent a shiver down Vikram's spine. "You've come this far. Don't stop now. Come. Let's find the truth."

The path led to the statue of Chendkai, its blackened stone looming like a sentinel in the moonlit clearing. The forest seemed to hum with an unnatural energy—the chorus of crickets and frogs blending into a strange, rhythmic cadence that resonated deep in Vikram's chest. Fireflies floated in erratic spirals around them, their fleeting light casting unsettling, shifting patterns on the ground.

Shyam walked past the statue without hesitation, his movements unnaturally smooth, his expression unreadable. Vikram followed, but as he approached the statue, a sudden chill gripped him. The air grew heavier, the rhythmic jungle song fading into a dissonant hum. His flashlight caught the carved features of the statue—a woman's face, stern and unforgiving. Just as he stepped closer, the statue's eyes seemed to glow, a deep crimson light that burned against the darkness.

"STOP, YOU FOOL! REMEMBER THE CURSE!"

The voice was thunderous, vibrating through the air as the statue's stone head turned toward him with a grating sound. Vikram stumbled back, his flashlight shaking in his hand. The light flickered erratically as if reacting to the oppressive energy radiating from the statue. The stone figure's gaze was piercing, alive, and filled with an ancient rage.

"Come on, brother," Shyam called from the other side, his voice calm and unaffected, as though he hadn't heard the warning.

Vikram's throat tightened. The urge to flee clawed at his mind, but an invisible force compelled him forward. Swallowing his fear, he stepped past the statue. Its head slowly turned back to its original position, but the warning echoed in his mind, carving itself into his thoughts.

They continued deeper into the jungle, where the trees parted to reveal a vast, still water body. The moonlight reflected off its glass-like surface, creating an eerie, mirror-like sheen. In the center of the water stood an island of jagged rocks, their dark forms rising ominously from the depths like a fortress. The air was deathly still, the silence broken only by their breaths and the faint lapping of water against the shore.

"You used to love swimming," Shyam said, his voice carrying an unnerving familiarity as he stepped into the water without hesitation. The ripples moved outward in perfect symmetry, too controlled, too deliberate.

Vikram hesitated, his flashlight scanning the water's edge. It was shallow here, but the island loomed far away. The water seemed darker than it should have been, its surface opaque despite the moonlight. Still, he followed, stepping into the cool water. It rose to his knees as he waded forward, his movements slow and deliberate. The chill seeped into his skin, and with each step, the weight of the forest seemed to press harder on him.

The climb up the rocks was treacherous. Shyam ascended with inhuman ease, his bare feet gripping the slick, jagged surface. Vikram struggled, the sharp edges biting into his palms and boots slipping on the moss-covered stone.

"Careful," Shyam said, his tone distant, almost amused, as Vikram reached for an unsteady rock.

It was too late. The rock gave way, and Vikram tumbled down, his body colliding with the uneven surface before landing hard on the cave floor below. Pain exploded through him, radiating from his back and shoulders. He gasped, his breath coming in shallow bursts.

"AHHH!" Vikram's scream tore through the oppressive silence as his body collided with the jagged rocks below. Pain erupted through his back and sides, sharp and searing, spreading like wildfire with every shallow breath he managed to draw. His head spun as he tried to focus, but his vision blurred, and the dim light of the cave swirled into disorienting patterns.

For a moment, he lay motionless, his chest rising and falling in ragged gasps. Each breath felt like a knife twisting in his ribs.

He tried to shift his position, to push himself up, but the sharp pain in his lower back froze him in place.

"Ah… damn it…" he muttered, his voice barely audible over the pounding of his heart. His hands clawed weakly at the rocky ground, seeking something solid to anchor himself, but every movement sent fresh jolts of agony shooting up his spine.

Minutes stretched into what felt like hours. The initial sharpness of the pain began to dull, replaced by a cold, creeping numbness that spread from his waist downward. A chill ran through him, more from realization than the damp air of the cave.

"No… no, no, no…" he whispered, his voice trembling. Panic swelled in his chest as he willed his legs to move, to respond. He tried to shift his foot, his ankle—anything—but the numbness held firm, like an invisible weight pinning him down.

"I… I can't…" His breath hitched as fear tightened its grip around his throat. "I can't feel my legs…"

Shyam appeared beside him, crouching with an unnatural stillness. His face remained calm, too calm. "Don't worry," he said softly, his voice almost a whisper. "You've reached the answer."

Vikram blinked through the haze of pain, his surroundings slowly coming into focus. The cave was otherworldly, unlike anything he had ever seen. The walls shimmered with phosphorescent green fungus, casting an ethereal glow that pulsed faintly, like a heartbeat. The ground was scattered with vibrant, otherworldly mushrooms, their colors vivid and alien. Moonlight filtered through cracks above, creating shifting patterns of light and shadow.

"This… this is it," Vikram whispered, his voice trembling as he fumbled for his GoPro. He turned it on, the faint beep breaking the silence. "Magic. This is the enchanted place. The plant Bhairav talked about—it must be here. Chendkai burned the forest, but it survived. Because of the water? The cave? Both? It's calling me… It's calling me."

Shyam knelt closer, his eyes glinting with an intensity that sent a shiver through Vikram. "Of course it's calling you," he said, his voice smooth, almost mocking. "Why else do you think you're here?"

Vikram turned to him, his breath catching as he noticed the subtle changes in Shyam's face. His brother's features seemed sharper, more angular, and his eyes gleamed with an unholy light. The smile that spread across Shyam's lips was predatory, stretching too wide, too unnatural.

Around them, the jungle seemed to shift, the air growing heavier with each passing second. The glowing mushrooms seemed to pulse in time with an invisible rhythm, and the cave walls seemed to close in, alive with unseen watchers. The weight of the forest pressed down on Vikram as the truth—or something close to it—began to unfold.

Vikram lay sprawled on the cold, jagged rock, the searing agony in his broken back radiating in relentless waves. Each shallow breath scraped against his ribs, but worse was the gnawing hunger that clawed at him, hollowing out his insides like a feral animal. The cave around him shimmered with an unsettling beauty—the walls alive with phosphorescent moss and clusters of mushrooms glowing in eerie, otherworldly hues. Moonlight trickled through the cracks above, bathing the chamber in a surreal, pale blue glow.

Shyam stood nearby, watching him with an unsettling calm, his lips curled into that same strange smile. Slowly, he crouched and plucked one of the mushrooms, its surface glistening in the dim light. Without hesitation, Shyam bit into it. The wet, tearing sound of the flesh echoed through the cave, sending an involuntary shiver down Vikram's spine.

Vikram's gaze locked onto the mushrooms scattered across the ground. His stomach churned, an insatiable hunger overriding his pain. The sight of Shyam eating only intensified the pull. His thoughts spiraled as he clung to fragments of logic to anchor himself. *Ever been outside a fast-food joint where the smell drags you in? They say companies add chemicals to make the smell irresistible. That's what this feels like.*

His trembling hand inched toward one of the mushrooms, its vibrant colors pulsing faintly, almost as though it were alive.

"Better to eat and risk it," he whispered to himself, his voice trembling, "than to die starving."

He plucked one from the ground. The instant it touched his fingers, the mushroom quivered, and before he could react, it exploded in his face. A burst of viscous slime coated his mouth and nose. Vikram gagged, his body convulsing as the slime slid down his throat. He coughed, trying to spit it out, but instinct betrayed him—he swallowed.

Sweetness flooded his mouth, a taste unlike anything he'd ever known. It was intoxicating, electric. A surge of warmth coursed through him, spreading from his core to his limbs. His fingers trembled as he reached for another mushroom. This time, he didn't hesitate. The slime burst as he shoved it into his mouth, dripping down his chin and onto the rock. Hunger demanded more. He grabbed handfuls, stuffing them into his mouth as the cave began to shift around him.

The glowing mushrooms blurred and stretched, their light no longer static but pulsing, throbbing like the heartbeat of the earth itself. Colors twisted and warped, bleeding into one another in slow-motion waves. The moss on the walls began to writhe, its green luminescence snaking like veins alive with energy.

Shyam's laughter cut through the surreal haze, loud and jarring. It echoed unnaturally, the sound bending and twisting as though the cave itself were joining in. He spun in a slow, exaggerated circle, his movements impossibly fluid, his face shifting in and out of focus like a figure in a dream.

Then another voice joined him, soft and melodic, humming a lullaby Vikram hadn't heard in decades. His heart twisted in his chest as his mother's hazy figure materialized beside Shyam, her sari glowing faintly in the kaleidoscopic light. She smiled at him, her lips moving soundlessly as if calling his name.

Vikram blinked rapidly, shaking his head to dispel the image, but it only grew clearer. His vision filled with shifting, overlapping layers of past and present. Shyam danced beside their mother, his hands outstretched as if pulling invisible strings.

And then, she appeared.

Nasreen, her body draped in a transparent white dress, moved toward him with feline grace. Her pale skin glowed faintly, her curves shimmering in the dim light.

"Damn, this is strong. I'm losing my sense of reality," Vikram muttered into his recorder, his voice slurred. "Whatever this is… it's good."

He crawled after Nasreen as she beckoned him with a seductive smile.

"Come to me…" her voice cooed, soft and sweet, cutting through the haze of his mind.

Shyam and their mother joined her, their voices overlapping in a hypnotic chant. "Come with us!"

Vikram dragged himself forward, his useless legs trailing behind him. The ground beneath him began to tilt and shift as if alive, forcing him to claw his way forward with his hands.

The water outside the cave had risen, creeping into the cave's entrance. It swirled around him, cold and unrelenting, soaking his body.

"I don't think this water is real," he muttered into the recorder, his words thick and distorted. "Like them… it's just an illusion. It's pushing me away, keeping me here!"

But the urge to follow them was stronger. With a surge of determination, he pulled his body over jagged rocks, ignoring the deep cuts forming on his arms and chest. His blood mingled with the water, creating a surreal swirl of red and blue beneath the moonlight.

Vikram broke free of the cave and plunged into the water outside. The cold enveloped him, dulling the searing pain in his back. The moonlight reflected on the surface, creating a surreal, shimmering glow. For a moment, he floated, his arms weakly treading water, before Nasreen appeared beneath him.

Her body moved gracefully through the water, her wet, translucent dress clinging to her pale skin. The curves of her breasts were perfectly outlined, shimmering under the fractured moonlight. She glided closer, her face tilted upward, her dark eyes locking with his as her lips parted slightly. Her hair spread out like dark silk, framing her otherworldly beauty.

Nasreen twisted in the water, floating on her back beneath him, her breasts breaching the surface momentarily before disappearing again. Her movements were slow, deliberate, hypnotic. She mirrored his position, her face mere inches below his, moving as though she were his reflection.

Vikram laughed, the sound bubbling up uncontrollably. His mind screamed that this wasn't real, but his body and senses betrayed him.

He pulled himself out of the water, collapsing on the muddy shore. His breath came in shallow, ragged gasps. His body felt light, detached, and his hunger gnawed at him like a beast.

Dragging himself forward, Vikram gripped his recorder tightly, the glowing mushrooms pulsing faintly at the edges of his vision, like mocking stars in a vast, uncaring void. He pressed the button, his voice barely a whisper but steady enough to be heard.

"The plant... the mushroom..." he rasped, each word a struggle against the weight of his failing body. "One of the ancient beings on Earth. It calls somehow. Maybe chemicals... pheromones. If only... if only I could test it in a lab..."

"Maybe it's dying..." his voice grew fainter. "It needs to grow. We're drawn to it... like fireflies to fire..."

He coughed violently, his chest heaving with the effort, but a faint, almost delirious smile crossed his cracked lips. "Beautiful... no pain..."

He paused, staring into the dark canopy above, the trees looming over him like silent judges. He pressed the recorder closer to his lips, his voice gaining a bitter edge. "Does it suffer, like us, from consciousness? Or is it just an automaton, playing its tricks, indifferent to what it destroys?" His eyes darted to the trees, their shadows twisting into towering specters in his mind.

"Are they all conscious? If not individually then collectively perhaps! Or is this jungle just a sprawling corpse, animated by mindless decay?" He chuckled weakly, a hollow, broken sound. "And even if it were conscious... why would it care? Why would it waste a thought on me, a fleeting speck in its endless, meaningless cycles?"

He let his head drop for a moment, staring at the dirt beneath him, feeling its cold embrace. "Maybe it's laughing. Or maybe it's pitying me. But why would it bother with either?"

A tremor rippled through his shattered body as he exhaled, his voice thinning to a fragile whisper. "Maybe their feelings are alien. Something we can't understand. Something beyond human emotions. Is that even possible?" His cracked lips twitched into a faint, bitter smile, the thought lingering like a shadow in his mind. "Or maybe it's not feelings at all. Just… something else entirely. Something we'll never grasp."

He let out a hollow chuckle, the sound quickly swallowed by the suffocating silence of the jungle. "Damn…"

His grip on the recorder loosened, his trembling hand falling to the ground. The jungle around him remained unmoved, its shadows deep and endless, the faint glow of the mushrooms pulsing like the heartbeat of something vast and indifferent.

The recorder captured the sound of his dragging body, the sloshing of mud, and his uneven breaths. He stopped briefly, his head hanging low. Then he pressed on, crawling across the unforgiving terrain.

A soft laugh escaped his lips, broken and delirious. "Nasreen… she's beauty. Ghosts… they must be… hallucinations." His voice cracked. "She isn't dead. How long… how long have I been here?"

His breathing grew heavier, his words slurring. "Is she… dead? I… I don't… t-think…"

The recorder fell from his hand, tumbling into the dirt. The faint glow of its red light flickered as Vikram crawled on, his movements growing weaker with each passing moment.

The hallucinatory figures returned, hovering at the edges of his vision. Shyam appeared again, walking beside him, his face calm and unreadable. Nasreen followed, her dress now dry and clinging to her body like a second skin. Her breasts rose and fell with each step, the curve of her body exaggerated by the surreal haze of Vikram's mind.

"Come with us," they whispered in unison, their voices harmonizing with the jungle's eerie symphony.

Vikram's stomach churned with hunger, a deep, gnawing ache that refused to be ignored. He looked around desperately, his vision spinning, searching for anything to eat. His brother crouched nearby, plucking leaves and chewing them with ease.

"Nature is full of food," Shyam said, his voice dripping with mockery.

Vikram's eyes darted to a frog hopping nearby. Without hesitation, he lunged at it, his hands clumsy and trembling. He caught it and bit down, the slick skin bursting in his mouth. The taste was foul, but he didn't care. He swallowed the pieces greedily, his hunger momentarily sated.

"I'm going mad," Vikram slurred, his words barely audible. "Mad... can't... speak..."

He crawled further, his energy draining with every movement. A green snake slithered across his path, its smooth body glinting in the faint light. He grabbed it with shaking hands, ignoring its frantic writhing. The snake bit him on the cheek, its fangs sinking deep, but Vikram felt no pain. He grinned, his lips curling into a delirious smile, and bit into the snake, swallowing it piece by piece.

His crawling slowed as the venom began to take hold. The jungle around him blurred, the vibrant colors of the mushrooms and fireflies blending into a kaleidoscope of light. He crawled for what felt like eternity, his body pushed to its limit.

Finally, he reached the base of a massive tree. Its roots curled outward like the arms of an ancient throne, welcoming him into its embrace. Vikram slumped against the trunk, his breath shallow and labored. The jungle seemed to quiet around him, the whispers fading into silence. He tired to adjust his GoPro mounted on his head, but his hands gave up.

With his last ounce of strength, he looked up at the moonlight filtering through the canopy. His lips curled into a faint smile, a fleeting moment of peace overtaking him.

Vikram died seated at the base of the tree, like a king on his throne, as the jungle swallowed him whole. Yet, the GoPro mounted on his head remained awake, its tiny red light blinking steadily. The camera lens, smeared with sweat and dirt, continued capturing the surreal landscape—the gnarled roots, the shifting shadows, and the silent sentinels of the night. It bore witness to his final moments, recording the jungle's eerie stillness, long after the man it belonged to had drawn his last breath.

The Professor's Trail

"If you don't know where you are going, any road can take you there."

– Alice's Adventures in Wonderland

"Are you okay?"

The voice, soft and melodious, sliced through the haze of his sleep. Sid stirred, his eyelids heavy and reluctant, before cracking open to the world around him. Morning light filtered through the dense canopy above, casting dappled patterns on the jungle floor. The air was cool, damp, and carried the earthy scent of moss and decay.

Leaning over him was a woman with deep brown skin, black eyes that seemed to draw him in, and sharp, well-defined features. Her chin was firm, her brows arched, and an innocence lingered in her expression that made her face disarmingly likable.

"Am I dreaming?" Sid murmured, his voice raw and scratchy.

"Not this time," she replied, a faint smile tugging at her lips.

Baburao stepped into view next, his silhouette towering behind her. The lines on his face were etched deeper in the soft morning light, worry plain in his expression.

Sid groaned as he shifted, the dull ache in his head flaring. He reached up and gingerly touched the spot where he'd hit the branch. The skin was tender, swollen, but there was no blood. His bike lay on its side nearby, the metal glinting faintly in the new day's light, a silent reminder of his crash.

"How long was I out?" Sid croaked, his voice thick with exhaustion.

"All night, probably," Baburao said. "We found you just after sunrise."

Sid's hand instinctively went to the Colt revolver at his side. Its weight brought a small measure of comfort. He leaned back against the tree, letting its rough bark press into his aching muscles, and eyed the two figures above him.

"Who are you?" he asked sharply, his tone edged with suspicion.

The three of them exchanged hurried stories. Maya handed Sid a water bottle, her movements fluid but deliberate. He took it without hesitation, gulping half of it in one go. The cool liquid soothed his parched throat and revived him slightly.

"So, you saw the ghosts?" Baburao asked cautiously, his tone careful, as though the word itself could summon them.

Sid's gaze turned distant, the memories of the night before flickering in his mind like a dying flame. "I don't know what I saw," he said quietly. "But we need backup. We should head to the village and get help."

Baburao shook his head firmly. "We are the backup. No one else will come here."

Sid frowned but didn't argue. "Let's check the car first," he said, pushing himself to his feet, his body protesting with every movement.

The walk back to the Verna took only a few minutes, but the tension among them was palpable, an almost physical presence pressing against their backs. The jungle seemed to tighten around them, its shadows sharp even in the growing sunlight.

Manoj's lifeless body still sprawled across the car's roof, a twisted and unchanging sight. Dark streaks of dried blood marred the windshield below him, the contrast against the red paint stark and unnerving. Sid circled the car, his sharp eyes scanning every inch.

"She was standing here," Sid said suddenly, pointing to a spot near the car. He crouched, examining the ground with the meticulousness of a predator hunting for clues. Leaves, mud—everything was undisturbed, untouched. No footprints. No evidence of anyone having stood there.

"How?" he muttered to himself, frustration thick in his voice.

The silence stretched taut between them, broken only by the jungle's morning symphony—the occasional birdcall, the distant rustle of leaves, the sound of their own measured breaths.

"We're here to find the professor," Maya said, her voice steady, almost resolute. "Maybe, in the process, we'll find Swati too."

"Why don't you join us?" Baburao asked Sid, his tone practical, almost detached.

Sid hesitated. The jungle loomed before them, dark and uninviting, even under the sun's tentative light. His eyes traced the footprints leading deeper into its depths, vanishing into the tangled undergrowth like whispers fading into silence. If Swati was alive, the answers lay in the jungle's maw.

With a short nod, he made his decision. "Fine."

The three of them left the muddy road and stepped into the jungle. Almost immediately, the air seemed to shift, growing heavier, thicker. The earthy scent of damp soil mingled with a metallic tang that set Sid's nerves on edge. Every snap of a twig and rustle of leaves felt amplified, as though the jungle itself was watching them, waiting for its moment to strike.

The further they went, the more the forest seemed to close in, its dense canopy darkening their path. The weight of the jungle pressed against them, each rustling leaf and snapping twig sending tendrils of unease through the group. The damp air carried a metallic tang, sharp and unsettling, as though the forest itself was alive and watching.

Sid paused briefly, glancing around the oppressive greenery, and took a deep breath. Then, tilting his head upward, he clasped his hands together and looked at the heavens.

"Lord Ganpati," he muttered dramatically. "I don't know if last night was the best of my life or the worst."

Baburao stopped and frowned, looking at Sid in confusion. "What are you talking about?"

Sid smirked, his expression lightening as he spread his hands theatrically. "Oh, you know. I closed my eyes with one beauty staring down at my face"—he paused for effect, glancing meaningfully at Baburao—"and opened them to another." He turned to Maya with a playful grin, his eyebrows waggling mischievously.

Maya tried to ignore but couldn't suppress a small smile.

Baburao shook his head, muttering something under his breath about city folks, but a faint smile tugged at the corner of his lips.

The jungle grew unnervingly quiet as they ventured deeper into its shadowy embrace. Baburao led the way with steady steps, his demeanor calm, almost reverent. Sid trailed behind, his thoughts a tangled mess of the previous night's events.

Swati.

She had been there—he was certain. But was she real? A ghost? His mind wrestled with the questions. If she was dead, was she calling for help? To find her body? And what about that twisted, jerking thing on the car? He shook his head, muttering a soft prayer under his breath as if to steady himself.

"Stop!" Baburao's sharp voice cut through his thoughts like a blade.

Sid blinked, snapping to attention. They had stopped before a towering, ten-foot statue of Chendkai. Ancient and dark, its stone surface was worn smooth by the jungle's relentless grip, vines snaking up its legs like veins feeding a heart of stone.

"Let's pray first," Baburao said, dropping to his knees with a solemn sincerity.

Without hesitation, Sid knelt, folding his hands and bowing his head with reverence. His lips moved in silent prayer, murmuring invocations to Goddess Chendkai. Beside him, Maya hesitated, glancing at the statue with a mixture of doubt and discomfort. Finally, she crouched, her posture half-hearted.

Minutes passed in tense silence, broken only by the faint rustle of leaves. Baburao's head remained bowed, his lips moving in inaudible prayer. Sid found solace in the act, a familiar ritual that offered a brief reprieve from the chaos swirling in his mind. Maya, however, shifted uncomfortably, her eyes darting around the clearing as if searching for an excuse to leave.

Finally, Baburao rose, brushing the dirt from his knees. "Alright," he said simply.

As they stood, the jungle seemed to exhale, a soft rustle rippling through the trees like a whispered warning.

Then came the sound—low, guttural, and resonant.

Sid froze, his hand instinctively going to the Glock at his side.

"What was that?" he whispered, his voice steady but tense.

Maya stiffened, her skepticism faltering. "What? I didn't hear anything. It's probably just an animal."

"Or maybe the spirits of the dead," Baburao said calmly, his gaze fixed ahead, unshaken.

The growl grew louder, morphing into something disturbingly like laughter before dissolving into the air. Sid's grip on the Glock tightened, but he didn't flinch.

"Here, take this," Baburao said, removing his tabeez and handing it to Sid.

"What about you?" Sid asked, accepting the amulet and glancing at Baburao.

Baburao shrugged, his face unreadable. "I'm already immune to this jungle. Ghosts seem to have accepted me."

"You should take mine," Maya offered, her tone tinged with sarcasm as she held up her amulet. "Anyway, I don't—"

"No," Sid cut her off sharply, his voice steady and authoritative. "You need to believe for it to work. Don't take it lightly."

Maya lowered her hand, caught off guard by the seriousness in his tone.

Baburao cast Sid a glance, a faint smile tugging at his lips. He remembered his exact same words to Vikram. "Hope she forgives us," Baburao murmured, casting one last look at the statue.

"Forgives us for what?" Sid asked, frowning slightly.

"Keep moving," Baburao replied, his voice firm but low. He stepped forward, the jungle swallowing him once again. As they walked, he began recounting the tale of Chendkai, his words weaving an eerie story that seemed to seep into the jungle around them, making every shadow feel alive.

As they left the clearing, Maya glanced back at the statue. For a fleeting moment, she thought she saw its stone eyes gleam faintly—a warning, or perhaps a silent farewell.

The image burned itself into her mind, vivid and unshakable, as though death itself had turned its gaze upon her.

"Don't react to voices or anything you see," Baburao said firmly, his voice low but commanding. He moved with purpose, his eyes scanning the forest floor, his steps deliberate. As an experienced tracker, he knew the jungle rarely lied. Though six months was a long time, it whispered its secrets through faint traces—disrupted vegetation, faded footprints, and other signs that time hadn't fully erased.

The jungle had done its best to reclaim the trail. Vines had crept over disturbed earth, leaves layered the ground, and broken branches had regrown. But Baburao's trained eyes found patterns in the chaos—subtle hints of past movement etched into the present.

"This takes more intuition than certainty," Baburao muttered, mostly to himself, as his keen gaze flitted over the forest floor.

They soon arrived at a clearing in the heart of the jungle. A shimmering water body stretched out before them, its calm surface reflecting the late afternoon sunlight. Baburao stopped abruptly at the edge, crouching to inspect the ground.

"He went into the water," Baburao murmured, tracing faint footprints leading to the edge.

"Why would anyone do that?" Sid asked, stepping closer.

"How do you know?" Maya's voice carried a note of skepticism.

Baburao gestured toward the marks, his tone matter-of-fact. "Look at the size and depth of the prints. Definitely boots— probably male boots." The damp clay held the faint outline of tread marks, like an impression suspended in time. Baburao's voice softened as he continued, almost as if addressing the forest itself. "The marks will last until the next rains wash them away."

Maya frowned but remained silent. Baburao rose, scanning the clearing with a sharp, practiced gaze. "This place would've looked very different six months ago."

"What do you mean?" Sid asked, raising an eyebrow.

Baburao pointed toward the water. "This is backwater from the dam they built recently. Before that, it might have been just a stream or a shallow pond. The water level rising… it changes everything."

As he spoke, something caught his eye—a dark shape barely visible beneath the water's surface. He squinted, tilting his head. "There's something submerged out there… a cave entrance? Or maybe an island that's now underwater."

Sid followed his gaze. "If he went out there, he's either drowned or…"

"Or he crawled out," Baburao finished, pointing to faint drag marks leading from the water's edge into the vegetation.

"He crawled?" Maya's skeptical tone softened into curiosity.

"Probably injured," Sid said. "Broken back, legs… or too weak to stand after starving."

Baburao checked the sky. The shadows stretched longer now; evening was settling in. The jungle at night was no place to be, but retreating now would waste precious time. He sighed. "We move quickly. No stopping."

Baburao resumed the trail, his movements brisk. Sid stayed close, his eyes darting to every shadow, his nerves taut. Maya followed with an uncharacteristic quiet, her usual skepticism tempered by unease. The jungle's oppressive silence gnawed at her resolve. Her hand unconsciously brushed the amulet around her neck. *Believe in it, and it will protect you*, she reminded herself. At this point, anyone would believe anything.

The tracks were faint, nearly nonexistent now. Baburao hesitated, frustration etched into his face. He didn't want to admit it, but the trail had grown cold. Six months was too long for even the jungle to remember. But he pushed forward, unwilling to show doubt.

"How did he know where to go?" Sid asked, his voice edged with suspicion. "Was he following something? Or someone?"

Baburao paused, his gaze distant. "Spirits," he muttered. "The jungle lures people."

Maya stopped in her tracks, narrowing her eyes. "Spirits?" she repeated, incredulous. "You're seriously saying ghosts guided him?"

Sid felt a chill crawl up his spine. "Lured… to what?" he murmured, his voice quieter. His mind raced. What if they were being lured too? Was Maya even real? Baburao? After last night, seeing Swati, he couldn't trust his own senses. He reached out and gripped Baburao's arm briefly, grounding himself.

"I don't know where," Baburao admitted, his voice taut. "But we'll find out."

Suddenly, he froze, pointing at something half-hidden by a bush. "There!"

Sid followed his gaze. Beneath the shadow of a sprawling tree trunk lay a small voice recorder, its metal surface scratched but intact.

Sid crouched and picked it up, inspecting it closely. "Battery's dead," he said flatly.

"Let's rest for a moment," Maya suggested, already pulling a power bank from her backpack.

Sid didn't argue. He sank to the ground beneath a tree, exhaustion weighing on him. He leaned back against the trunk.

Sid was used to being the main character in every narrative, the one who led and dictated the course of events. But now, watching Baburao take charge with unwavering confidence, he couldn't help but feel a pang of jealousy. Even with his overweight frame, Baburao moved with surprising stamina, seemingly untouched by the fatigue that clung to Sid like a second skin.

Baburao hesitated. The sky was darkening, and every instinct screamed at him to keep moving. But he relented. "Five minutes," he said sternly, his tone leaving no room for negotiation.

The jungle seemed to shift as they sat, its shadows thickening. The air grew heavy, carrying the faint metallic scent of damp earth and decay. Maya connected the recorder to the power bank, her fingers moving quickly. The red light blinked once, signaling it had turned on.

Baburao scanned the surroundings, unease etched into his features. They were too close now—close to something the jungle wanted them to find.

And for the first time, even Baburao wasn't sure they'd survive the night.

Maya pressed play on the recorder again. The static crackled, and Vikram's voice emerged, hoarse and trembling.

"I… I don't know how long I've been here. Hours? Days? Time feels… strange. I'm deeper now. Too deep. There's no turning back. But… but he's here. My brother. Shyam."

His voice faltered, the weight of emotion palpable.

"He found me… in this place. But it doesn't make sense. He… he died years ago. And yet, he knows everything. Every thought. Every secret. Like he's been with me all along."

The recording clicked, then resumed, quieter and more frantic.

"It's not him. It can't be him. He's... me. That's why he knows. He's a reflection, pulled from my mind by this... this place. The jungle. It's in my head now. Twisting it, turning my own thoughts against me."

Vikram's breathing grew heavier, his words more disjointed.

"He's a hallucination. A perfect mirror. Everything I know, he knows. Every doubt, every fear... he reflects it back at me. He's guiding me, but... but where? To what?"

A burst of static cut through the recording, followed by a faint sound—a distant whisper, barely audible.

"I think... I think the jungle wants me to believe in him. To trust him. But he is me... and I am going crazy!"

Another pause, filled with ragged breaths and rustling. Then, Vikram's voice dropped to a whisper.

"If you find this... if you hear this... remember: the jungle will use you against yourself. It will show you what you want to see, what you fear, what you desire. Don't trust anyone... not even yourself."

The recorder clicked off, leaving a chilling silence in its wake.

Maya's fingers trembled as she pressed play again, and Vikram's voice resumed, softer now, trembling with awe and dread.

"I—I found it. The cave... it's not just... No, no, I have to keep going. It's beautiful, but—"

The recorder hissed, and the audio cut off abruptly. Sid flinched at the sharp burst of static, his hand instinctively brushing the Glock at his side.

The voice resumed, softer still. *"The mushrooms... they glow. They... call you. I can feel them... in my head. I can't—"*

Another jarring burst of static, followed by a faint, unidentifiable sound. It was distant yet unnerving, like a whisper carried on the wind.

"What the hell was that?" Sid asked, his eyes darting around the dense jungle.

"Shhh," Baburao murmured, his voice tense. His attention remained fixed ahead, but his pace slowed.

Maya glanced nervously at the recorder, her unease growing. The device crackled again, and Vikram's voice returned, his words clipped and hurried.

"If you're listening… don't trust the voices. Don't trust… her. Check the camera. I can see Shyam, I can see her through the camera, can you? I can… because… you know…"

"Her?" Maya whispered, her brow furrowing. She looked at Sid, who avoided her gaze, his thoughts clearly elsewhere.

Before anyone could speak, the recorder played a new sound—ragged breathing, followed by the faint crunch of footsteps. Then, Vikram's voice, lower this time, almost a whisper.

"She's not… she's not dead. She can't be dead. But… but she's not alive, either. Oh god… oh no… she's looking at me. Nasreen…beautiful…"

At the mention of the name, Maya felt a surge of jealousy, unbidden but sharp. The recorder clicked off again. The trio stood frozen, the oppressive silence of the jungle now louder than any sound.

So this was it. The mythical plant tied to the goddess. Dormant for centuries, it had waited in the shadows of the cave. The flooding caused by the dam must have triggered something—a survival instinct deeply embedded in its existence. Perhaps the water had awakened a preprogrammed plan, forcing the plant to act. It grew, spreading its influence, luring victims to its grasp like a predator using bait. And Vikram, drawn by his relentless search for truth, had followed it to the end.

The jungle seemed to pulse with life, the growing darkness sharpening every sound. The fiery red sky above bled through the canopy, casting long, distorted shadows. The oppressive stillness around them was a warning—a silent signal of the night ahead.

Baburao stood abruptly, his eyes scanning the clearing. "We need to leave," he said, breaking the silence. His tone was firm, almost urgent.

Sid frowned, frustration simmering. "We're so close," he muttered, reluctant to leave the trail.

Baburao didn't respond immediately. He adjusted his bag and glanced at the sky, his face grim. Evening was near, and with it came the jungle's darkest secrets. The spirits would stir soon, their presence impossible to ignore.

Maya, practical as always, dismissed the notion. Hallucinations. That was all this was. The professor's voice had explained it clearly—pheromones, or perhaps a chemical in the air. A biological reaction, not the supernatural. Yet the oppressive atmosphere of the forest made even her doubts waver. She touched the tabeez around her neck, more for comfort than belief.

"Why doesn't it affect Baburao?" she wondered. The answer came quickly to her mind: his old brain surgery. An accident during college had left him changed, and perhaps that change had granted him immunity. Science often worked in strange, unpredictable ways.

A sudden shift in the atmosphere made them all pause. The jungle, already unnervingly quiet, seemed to hold its breath. Then they saw her.

Swati.

She stood partially concealed behind a thick tree trunk, her torn dress revealing patches of dirt, dried blood, and fungal growth creeping along her skin. Her wide, unblinking eyes locked onto them, cold and alien. It had only been three days since she disappeared, yet her appearance told a different story—one of decay and years spent in the jungle's cruel embrace.

Sid froze, his breath catching in his throat. "Am I hallucinating?" he whispered, his voice shaky, almost pleading for reassurance.

Maya didn't answer immediately, her own eyes riveted on the figure. After a beat, she muttered, "I guess me too," her voice tinged with doubt and disbelief.

Baburao, however, remained steady. "She's real," he said firmly, stepping forward with cautious deliberation. His tone was calm, but his body betrayed the tension coursing through him—each step measured, as though the ground itself might shift beneath him.

He raised his hands in a gesture of peace. "We're here to help you," he said softly, his voice carrying an unshaken conviction.

Swati tilted her head, her movements unnaturally slow and deliberate. She stepped forward, her bare feet silent against the forest floor. There was no urgency in her gait, no visible sign of fear or distress—just an unnerving calm that sent chills down Sid's spine.

Something was wrong. Sid felt it in his gut, a primal instinct screaming louder with each step Swati took. She didn't move like someone in need of help. If anything, it felt as though *they* were the ones in danger.

His fingers brushed the Colt at his side, the weight of the weapon momentarily grounding him in the surreal reality. "Swati, are you alright?" he asked, his voice tight, almost trembling.

She didn't respond. Her silence was louder than any scream, her unblinking eyes fixed on him with an unsettling intensity. She took another step closer, her movements precise, deliberate, and disturbingly unnatural.

Sid hesitated, torn between stepping forward and retreating. His breath hitched as a faint rustling sound drifted through the air—like dry leaves stirring, but too deliberate, too calculated.

Maya's gaze darted upward, and her unease transformed into outright fear. "Sid, look up!" she shouted, her voice sharp, cutting through the oppressive stillness.

Sid's eyes snapped upward just as a shadow hurtled down from the canopy. He ducked instinctively, the Colt sliding smoothly from its holster into his grip. Beside him, Baburao stumbled backward with a startled cry, his footing faltering as he fought to steady himself.

Swati moved then. She lunged at Sid with terrifying speed, her body a blur of motion, her precision almost mechanical. Her torn dress fluttered in the dim light as she closed the gap between them with impossible agility.

Sid hit the ground and rolled, his gun trained on the figure that had landed just feet from Baburao. It was Kamlesh.

The sight was ugly. His body twisted unnaturally, his limbs contorted as he crawled on all fours like a giant, skittering spider. His wide, unblinking eyes fixed on Baburao with a predator's hunger, glinting unnaturally in the moonlight.

Sid didn't hesitate. The gunshot echoed like a thunderclap, shattering the jungle's oppressive silence. Kamlesh crumpled to the ground, a dark stain spreading across his stomach where the bullet struck.

But it wasn't over.

Swati, now crouched beside Sid, darted into the undergrowth with an inhuman burst of speed. Her shredded dress snagged on the bushes as she vanished into the shadows. Kamlesh, clutching his wound, began to crawl after her, dragging his broken body across the dirt with relentless determination.

"Catch them! Stop him!" Sid yelled, his voice raw with urgency.

But Baburao and Maya stood frozen, their faces pale, their bodies paralyzed by the surreal horror unfolding before them.

Sid scrambled to his feet, his heart pounding in his chest, but it was already too late. Swati and Kamlesh had disappeared into the dense jungle, leaving behind only the faint rustling of leaves and the suffocating silence of the clearing.

For a long moment, none of them spoke. The jungle seemed to breathe around them, its shadows pressing in as though it had swallowed Swati and Kamlesh whole. Above them, the night had fallen, and the full moon bathed the world in its cold, unrelenting glow.

The Goddess's Command

*"To fear the unknown is to be human,
but to embrace it is to touch the divine."*

– Unknown

The village square buzzed with an uneasy silence as Ramu Kaka paced back and forth, glancing toward the dense jungle that loomed on the horizon. The sun hung low in the sky, casting long shadows that crept across the clearing. It was 4:00 pm, and dusk was only two hours away.

Baburao was supposed to have returned by now. The plan was clear—find Vikram by noon if possible, and if not, bring back the sacred mud from the feet of Goddess Chendkai. Everything else had been arranged: the ritual materials were laid out, and Bhairav stood with Savitri at the edge of the square, ready to begin.

Bhairav already held the machete in one hand, its blade sharp and shiny. It was meant to be used for the hen's sacrifice during the ceremony, but now it seemed like a weapon as much as a tool.

But without the sacred mud, none of it could proceed.

"Damn that Baburao," Ramu muttered, his frustration barely contained. "He's never serious, even in times like this."

Villagers murmured among themselves, their anxiety growing. Despite Ramu's words, they all knew Baburao was brave—perhaps too brave. But this time, Ramu's irritation was tinged with genuine worry. He had pushed Baburao and the new guest Maya into the unknown. Anything happening to them was his responsibility.

"Hope he's alright," he added, his voice softer. His gaze shifted toward the jungle. "And that girl with him… Maya, right?

What if—" He stopped himself, unwilling to voice his darker thoughts.

Ramu turned back to the crowd, his eyes scanning for any sign of courage among them. "We need volunteers. Someone must go after then," he said firmly.

The villagers exchanged uneasy glances, their silence an answer in itself.

"We cannot postpone the ceremony, can we?" Ramu asked, his voice tinged with desperation.

Bhairav shook his head. "No. The goddess will not wait. The ceremony must be completed tonight."

The weight of those words settled heavily over the crowd.

"What do we do then?" one villager asked, his voice betraying his fear. "If Baburao doesn't return, there's no ritual, and if there's no ritual…"

"Enough!" Ramu barked. He looked at Bhairav, who stood silently with the machete hanging at his side, his grip tightening on the worn handle. His eyes were fixed on Savitri, whose expression remained steady despite the tension.

"I'll bring the mud," Bhairav said suddenly, his voice calm but resolute.

The crowd gasped, their murmurs rising again.

"It's too risky now," Ramu cautioned, stepping toward him. "You know the jungle at this hour—spirits stir before dusk. And we've already lost too many…"

Bhairav raised the machete slightly, its dull edge glinting faintly in the fading light. "We have no choice. If we don't complete the ritual tonight, the goddess's anger will only grow. It is still two hours to dark. I will go and return quickly."

Ramu hesitated, glancing at Savitri. Her expression was calm, her eyes steady. She gave him a small nod, her trust in her husband unshaken.

The villagers murmured again, this time more in agreement. Even Ramu, for all his caution, couldn't deny the logic.

"Alright," he said finally. "But if anything happens—if you see anything—you turn around and come straight back. No heroics, understood?"

"Understood," Bhairav said, his voice unwavering.

Ramu looked at him for a long moment, then clapped him on the shoulder. "Be quick, and may the goddess protect you."

Without another word, Bhairav turned and began walking toward the jungle, the machete still in his grip. The villagers watched in silence as his figure grew smaller against the vast green expanse.

The shadows of the trees stretched further, their edges blurring as the light began to fade.

Bhairav walked with purpose, chanting mantras under his breath. The rhythmic syllables, ancient and sacred, kept his focus as he ventured deeper into the jungle. The machete in his hand glinted faintly in the waning light, its weight grounding him. His faith in the goddess was steadfast, but a shadow of doubt lingered in his mind.

If Vikram, and now Baburao and Maya, have already crossed the goddess, what good is praying now? he thought. *Perhaps the curse is already broken, beyond repair.*

Still, he clung to the hope that the goddess might show mercy. If she was merciful enough, she might forgive them all.

The towering figure of Goddess Chendkai emerged ahead, her 10-foot stone statue looming in the clearing like an eternal sentinel. Bhairav knelt before her, placing the machete beside him as he folded his hands in reverence. The cool dirt pressed against his knees as he bowed his head, whispering fervent prayers for forgiveness.

As he prayed, faint particles floated in the air, catching the fading sunlight. They glittered like specks of gold, dancing lazily on the breeze. Bhairav didn't notice them at first, too focused on his chants. When he finally did, he assumed it to be dust stirred by the wind, though its shimmer was strangely mesmerizing.

After several minutes, he reached out and scooped the sacred dirt from the goddess's feet into a small cloth pouch. Tears welled in his eyes as he looked up at her imposing figure, his voice trembling as he spoke. "Mother, forgive us. Spare them, and the village."

As he rose, something shifted.

The statue moved.

Bhairav froze, his breath caught in his chest as the goddess's head tilted. Stone lips cracked open, and sand and dirt spilled from her face, cascading like a small landslide. Insects poured from the crevices, scattering in all directions.

"*Fool*," a deep, resonant voice thundered, sending vibrations through the ground beneath him. "*What use is praying to me now?*"

Bhairav dropped to his knees again, awe and terror warring in his heart. His head bowed low, his forehead nearly touching the dirt.

"*Praying will result in nothing*," the goddess continued, her voice like the rumble of a distant storm. "*Go get those people out of the jungle. As long as they remain inside, the curse persists.*"

Her head shook, dust and debris falling from her stone shoulders. The jungle around him seemed to hold its breath, the oppressive silence broken only by her words.

"Mother, are you commanding me to go into the jungle?" Bhairav asked, his voice small and trembling.

"*I am commanding you*," she roared, the power in her voice making the trees shiver. "*Stop this nonsense and go inside. Find those fools and drag them out.*"

Her words echoed through the clearing as she added, "*Do it quickly. I will be with you.*"

Then, silence.

The statue's head returned to its original position, her face still and lifeless once more. The glittering particles lingered in the air, their movement oddly deliberate. For a moment, Bhairav thought they formed faint shapes, shifting like whispers on the edge of his vision. But when he blinked, they were just specks again, drifting lazily.

Bhairav rose shakily to his feet, tears streaming down his cheeks. After years of prayers and devotion, the goddess herself had spoken to him. The moment felt surreal, overwhelming. He thought of running back to the village to share the miracle with everyone—especially Savitri, who had been the most devout among them.

But her command was clear. That could wait.

As he turned to leave the clearing, the jungle seemed to shift around him. The air felt lighter, almost inviting. The glittering particles grew denser, catching the dim light and creating a surreal glow. The path ahead appeared clearer, as though the jungle itself were guiding him forward.

The faint cries of birds blended into a gentle hum, almost melodic, as though the forest were encouraging his steps. The undergrowth parted easily, and the trees seemed to lean back, their branches allowing light to filter through.

Bhairav gripped the machete tightly as he stepped past the statue and into the shadows of the jungle. His breath steadied as he felt an odd sense of reassurance, as though unseen hands were guiding his steps.

But if he had paused to think—to truly question—he might have noticed how the jungle's whispers matched his own doubts and desires, subtly pulling him deeper.

Her words echoed in his mind: *Find them. Drag them out.*

With renewed determination, he pressed deeper into the jungle, the glittering particles dancing around him like silent guides.

The Ecstasy of Decay

"Decay is the beginning of all birth, the cradle of all life."

– Paracelsus

Swati sprinted through the undergrowth, her movements fluid and unnaturally fast. She stopped at the base of a towering tree and, with effortless grace, began climbing. Her fingers dug into the bark, her powerful muscles propelling her upward until she perched on a sturdy branch. She crouched there, her dark eyes scanning the forest floor below.

Kamlesh stumbled into view, dragging his twisted body across the ground. His movements were sluggish, his strength waning. Blood oozed from the gunshot wound in his stomach, leaving a dark trail behind him. Swati watched silently, her head tilting as a faint flicker of something human sparked in her mind.

Somewhere deep within her, the remnants of her rational mind still existed. That small, buried part of her wanted to scream for help, to call out to Sid and the others below. She wanted to join them, to escape this nightmare and return to the city. But that fragile voice was drowned by a more dominant force—a singular, overwhelming purpose.

The thoughts weren't hers anymore. They were the jungle's. The source had claimed her, wrapping her mind in a web of control. Her mission was clear: to protect the source and draw more humans to it. To convert them. And the reward? Pleasure.

Swati exhaled, her senses sharper than ever. The darkness below wasn't an obstacle; she could see through it, her vision clearer than before. Her body thrummed with power—her muscles pulsing, her strength boundless. She could leap, run, climb; she was unstoppable.

Then, it started again.

A sharp sting pricked her arm, and she glanced down. A pale, slender stalk of fungus was pushing through her skin, emerging from beneath the flesh. A small jet of blood followed, trickling down her arm, but there was no pain. Instead, there was something worse—pleasure. A wave of raw, uncontrollable ecstasy surged through her, drowning every other sensation.

Her skin twitched unnaturally as more fungal growths pushed out from under the surface, their tendrils curling and weaving like living things. The sensation of her own body betraying her should have horrified her, but the jungle's influence twisted it into something she couldn't resist.

She shuddered as the feeling reached its peak, her body trembling with an ecstasy that defied description. It was like an orgasm but magnified a hundredfold, coursing through every nerve, every cell. The pleasure was intoxicating, alien—too powerful to be human.

Her head tilted back, and a moan escaped her lips—low, guttural, and unrestrained. The jungle seemed to amplify the sound, carrying it through the trees like a haunting melody. Swati's fingers gripped the tree bark tightly as her body convulsed, her rational mind screaming for control, only to be smothered by the jungle's will.

Down below, the trio froze.

The moan drifted through the trees, carrying with it a strange and unsettling intimacy. It was unmistakably human, but its raw, primal edge made it unnatural.

Sid stopped mid-sentence, his hand instinctively tightening around his Colt. Maya clutched her tabeez, her knuckles white, her eyes darting around the dense shadows. Baburao stood still, his face tense, his gaze fixed on the canopy above.

"What was that?" Sid asked, his voice barely above a whisper.

No one answered.

The silence stretched, the jungle seeming to close in around them. The faint rustle of leaves in the wind and the distant hum of insects only heightened the unease.

Maya shifted closer to Baburao, her grip on the tabeez tightening. Her skepticism wavered under the weight of her fear. "It's… it's nothing," she murmured, but her voice lacked conviction.

"It didn't sound like nothing," Sid replied, his eyes scanning the darkness, his pulse quickening.

Above them, hidden in the tree, Swati's lips curled into a faint smile. The human part of her mind whispered again, desperate for freedom, but it was too late. The jungle had her now, and its will was hers.

Swati crawled down the tree and darted into the dense undergrowth. Her movements were fluid, animalistic, her senses heightened as the jungle seemed to guide her. Behind her, Kamlesh followed, dragging his twisted form across the forest floor, the red-green ichor dripping steadily from his wounds. Swati's mind was singular in its purpose: reach the source. Protect it at all costs.

The enemy was coming. Three humans. One with a gun.

The jungle's oppressive silence was broken only by the crunch of leaves underfoot and the occasional rustle of unseen creatures. The air felt heavier now, thick with humidity and an indefinable musk. Sid wiped sweat from his brow, his grip tightening on the Colt at his side.

Maya glanced at the ground, her sharp eyes scanning the faint tracks left in the soil. "These trails… they're all leading inward," she murmured.

Baburao nodded. "The forest guides its own. Always has."

Sid, walking just behind them, frowned. "Guides? You make it sound like the jungle is alive."

Maya shot him a look. "It is alive. You've heard of the fungal networks, right? How trees communicate through mycelium?"

Sid gave a hesitant nod. "Sure, like those nature documentaries. Trees sharing nutrients, warning each other about pests."

"Exactly," Maya continued. "But that's only part of it. Fungi don't just interact with trees—they connect entire ecosystems. Animals, plants... even us, in some ways. And we barely understand how deep those connections go."

Baburao, who had stopped to examine a broken branch, added without looking up, "In these jungles, everything listens. Everything responds."

Sid shook his head. "But this—" He gestured around them, his voice rising slightly. "This isn't some documentary. Swati, and the guy we shot—they're acting like animals. Like predators."

Maya slowed her pace, her gaze distant. "Fungi like *Ophiocordyceps* can manipulate their hosts in terrifying ways. It's not far-fetched to think something here evolved to do the same. Maybe not just to insects... but to us."

Sid stared at her. "Are you saying Swati is controlled by... a mushroom?"

Maya hesitated, then sighed. "I don't know. Maybe it's pheromones. Maybe it's a neurotoxin we haven't identified. Or maybe the jungle itself is more than just a collection of organisms." *"It is conscious... if not alone, then collectively?"* Vikram's recorded message echoed in her mind, each word twisting her thoughts into dark, tangled knots. A cold sweat broke across her skin as she scanned her surroundings. The trees weren't just looming—they were watching. Silent. Ancient. Waiting.

Her gaze dropped to the ground, and a sickening realization hit her. Beneath the earth, an intricate web of fungi connected every tree in the jungle, a vast, pulsating brain buried in the dirt. She could almost feel it, alive and thinking, plotting beneath her feet. The weaponized mushrooms—those cursed things—they weren't just a product of nature. They were tools, precise and deliberate. Their spores invaded, corrupted, enslaved. Animals. Humans. Nothing was safe.

Her breathing quickened, each sound from the jungle now more sinister than before. Was the rustle of leaves just the wind? Or something crawling, creeping, hunting?

The thought clawed at her mind: with centuries of torment—forests burned, creatures slaughtered, ecosystems desecrated—had nature finally turned its wrath upon humanity? Was the jungle not just alive, but vengeful?

Her stomach churned as the trees seemed to lean closer, their gnarled branches reaching like skeletal hands. The shadows between them deepened, filled with unspoken malice. The jungle wasn't just plotting. It was coming.

Her face went pale, her knees weak, as she felt the suffocating grip of a predator that didn't need claws or fangs—it had already claimed the air she breathed, the ground she stood on. There was no escape.

She fell silent, glancing up at the canopy, where shafts of golden light pierced through the thick green leaves. A faint glitter seemed to drift in the air, catching the light like motes of gold.

"What's that?" Sid asked, pointing at the shimmering particles.

Baburao squinted. "Spores, maybe. Or dust."

"Or something worse," Maya muttered under her breath.

The trio moved cautiously, their eyes darting between the trees and the faint glitter in the air. Sid felt a strange tingle in his chest, like static electricity. He thought back to Swati's eyes, the way they gleamed with something both alive and alien.

"Sid!"

The voice floated down from the trees, soft yet commanding, pulling his attention upward. A middle-aged woman in a blue saree stood amidst the foliage, her silhouette framed by dappled sunlight filtering through the leaves.

Sid froze, his breath caught in his throat. He blinked, and the figure stepped forward, her features unmistakable.

"Mother," he whispered, his voice breaking. Tears welled up in his eyes, and his body trembled.

His mother had died just months ago, her body ravaged by liver cancer that had metastasized to her lungs and kidneys. The endless cycles of therapy, chemo, and futile hope had left her frail, her spirit crushed long before her body gave out. Sid had watched helplessly as she withered away—a shell of the vibrant woman who had once cared for him.

The guilt never left him. No amount of rationalizing could quiet the nagging thought: *I could have done more.* It was the cruel burden of survival, the sin of being alive when someone you love is taken.

But now, standing before him, she was not the fragile figure etched into his memory. She was young again, radiant, her face glowing with health. She was his mother as she had been in her prime—when laughter lit her eyes, and her touch brought comfort.

Sid took a hesitant step forward, tears spilling freely. "Mother…"

Before he could move any further, Baburao's firm hand gripped his arm. "She isn't real," Baburao said, his voice steady but urgent.

Sid turned to him, his expression a mix of confusion and pain. He nodded slowly, his voice cracking as he said, "Does that matter?" He turned back to the figure, his tears flowing unchecked. "She is here!"

Baburao's grip tightened. "Sid, this jungle is messing with your head. Don't—"

"She's young," Sid interrupted, his gaze fixed on the woman in front of him. "Like I remember her... from childhood." His voice trembled. "Just once, I want to hold her like this again. The jungle gave me that. It gave me this chance."

Baburao's face contorted with concern. "This isn't a gift. It's a trap."

Sid shook his head, his resolve soft but unyielding. "Then it's a beautiful one!"

He pulled free of Baburao's grasp and ran toward the figure.

Behind them, Maya stood frozen, her wide eyes darting between Sid and the empty space where she saw only jungle.

She clutched her tabeez, though her rational mind resisted the idea of its power. She forced herself to focus, to analyze, repeating inwardly:

It's not real. Trust your senses. It's not real.

But Sid wasn't listening to reason.

His mother smiled, soft and familiar, her hand outstretched in a beckoning gesture.

Sid ran.

He grabbed her in his arms, holding on as if letting go would mean losing her all over again. She felt real—real to him.

His sobs wracked his body, his grip tightening as he clung to her like a child seeking solace.

"How are you, Mother? I have missed you so much."

His voice cracked, heavy with years of longing.

She just hugged him tighter, her hands moving over his head the way she always had.

Sid shuddered, breathing in the scent of her, his heart hammering. This was real. This had to be real.

"I'm getting married, Ma… in June." His voice wavered, thick with emotion. "Remember Kavita? She finally agreed."

He gave her the news, desperate to share this piece of his life with her.

His mother smiled down at him, her fingers brushing through his hair, warm, familiar.

"I'm so happy for you."

She kissed his forehead.

And for the first time in years, Sid felt whole.

Baburao cursed under his breath and turned to Maya. "Do you see her?"

"Nothing. He's hugging nothing!" she replied, her voice tinged with awe and fear. She squeezed the tabeez tighter, her lips set in a thin line as she fought to maintain her composure.

The jungle seemed to hum around them, the air thick with unseen forces. Every rustle of leaves, every whisper of wind carried a weight, as if the jungle itself were alive, watching. Maya tried to steady her breathing, her fingers pressing tightly against her tabeez. Her mind raced, forcing herself to repeat the mantra she had adopted: *Logic. Reason. Nothing else.*

But then she saw her.

Geeta.

The little girl stood just ahead, framed by the trees, her hand raised in a friendly wave. She wore her school uniform, the familiar green skirt and white shirt that Maya remembered so vividly. Her long hair was tied back with ribbons, and the large school bag slung over her shoulders seemed far too heavy for her small frame.

Maya froze.

Her breath caught in her throat as the memories surged back—Geeta's laughter, her mischievous smile, the way she always waited for Maya at the school gate. Geeta had been her best friend, her first real friend.

And then, the memory shifted—deeper, more personal, buried under years of silence.

The day she kissed her.

Her one and only kiss.

The whispering. The giggling after. The way Geeta had touched her lips, eyes wide, then grinned like she had discovered something wonderful.

Maya had never spoken about it. Not to anyone. Not even to herself.

Because two weeks later, Geeta was gone.

Like Sid and everyone else who survives, Maya too suffered the strange burden of living on when someone you love is lost.

But Geeta was not the only one.

She had lost everyone—her mother, her father.

She had no one left.

She was probably the worst in the lot— because while others mourned a piece of themselves, she had been hollowed out completely.

Her grip on the tabeez tightened, her knuckles white.

Logic. Reason. Nothing else, she repeated in her mind.

But she wanted to run to her. Grab her, hold her, kiss her again.

What did it matter if Geeta was a hallucination?

If life itself was a dream, then what was wrong with loving a hallucination inside it?

A dream within a dream.

Yet, she held herself back.

She couldn't lose her reason.

She reminded herself again.

Her heart raced as she forced herself to glance at Baburao, who was still pulling Sid away from the figure of his mother.

"Come with me, Sid," his mother commanded softly, her voice warm yet insistent as she began to walk deeper into the jungle.

Sid hesitated, his feet rooted to the ground. He looked back at Maya and Baburao, his eyes pleading.

"What?" Baburao asked sharply.

"She's asking me to follow her," Sid said, his voice trembling.

Maya's gaze darted back to Geeta.

The little girl waved again, her innocent smile unchanged, untouched by time, as if urging Maya to follow.

"*She's not real*," Maya whispered to herself, forcing the words out through gritted teeth.

But Geeta looked so real.

Her hands were shaking now. Tears pricked at her eyes, blurring the figure before her.

She rubbed them hard, pretending to clean the dirt.

"Where will she take us?" Maya asked suddenly, ignoring Geeta and focusing on Sid's mother.

Sid turned to the figure of his mother. "Where, Mother?" he asked, his voice a mix of curiosity and longing.

"To your destiny," she replied, her voice steady, unyielding.

The trio hesitated, the weight of the moment pressing down on them.

"Maybe that's where the source is," Maya said, her voice low but firm, as if convincing herself as much as the others.

Baburao glanced at her, his expression unreadable. He finally nodded, though his unease was palpable.

Sid checked his Colt, ensuring it was ready, then took a tentative step forward. His mother waited patiently, her figure almost glowing in the dappled sunlight filtering through the canopy.

Maya clenched her jaw and ignored Geeta's unwavering presence. The little girl had turned and was walking in the same direction as Sid's mother, her school bag bouncing lightly with every step.

Maya swallowed hard and followed, her gaze fixed firmly ahead. But no matter how much she tried to dismiss it, she could feel Geeta's small figure trailing beside her, just out of reach.

A little further into the jungle, they encountered the body of Kamlesh. He was sprawled on the ground, lifeless, with a grotesque mix of red and green blood oozing from his gunshot wound. The infection had spread rapidly; his skin was severely deformed, riddled with lesions. His head was completely bald, and small fungal pores had taken root across his body, their white stalks breaking through the skin like parasitic invaders.

The trio stood still, with the ghostly figures of Sid's mother and Geeta lingering silently behind them.

"We need to dispose of the body," Baburao said, his voice firm.

"How?" Maya replied, her gaze fixed on the monstrous sight. "We can't bury it."

"No, we have to burn it," Baburao said, his tone resolute. "Fire cleanses everything."

"What was the name of that fungus you mentioned?" Sid asked, his eyes narrowing as he studied the body.

"Ophiocordyceps," Maya said softly, as if the name itself carried an ominous weight.

Sid crouched next to the corpse, using his Colt to turn Kamlesh's head, which had been facing the ground. The sight made him recoil slightly. The eyes—if they could still be called that—were bulging out, stretched to their limits, their once-white sclera now veined with green and bluish lines. The pupils were gone entirely, leaving hollow, lifeless orbs.

"Are they blind?" he asked, his voice low, as if afraid of disturbing something unseen.

"No idea," Baburao replied, his expression grim.

"We don't have much time," Baburao continued, stepping closer. "We find the source, and then we burn everything down." His tone carried the weight of finality.

"Otherwise, the infection will spread throughout the jungle," he added, his worry evident.

"It must already have," Maya said, her voice tinged with dread. She looked around at the dense foliage, imagining the infection weaving its way through the ecosystem.

"What about the animals?" Sid asked, glancing toward the shadows of the jungle. "Aren't they infected too?"

The group exchanged uneasy glances, the possibility settling over them like a heavy shroud.

His mother waved at him again, her gesture gentle but insistent, as if beckoning him to move forward. Sid felt a pull deep within him, an urge that defied logic. Even without the infection, the fungus seemed to have a grip on his mind.

"We don't know," Baburao said finally, breaking the silence. "We assume the worst and do our best." He exhaled sharply. "For now, let's move on."

He fixed his gaze on Sid, making it clear that their path depended on him. It was Sid who could see his mother, and it was she who seemed to lead them to the source.

Sid hesitated for a moment, then nodded. Without a word, he began following the ethereal figure of his mother, her form gliding through the jungle with an unsettling grace. The others trailed behind, their steps heavy with unease.

Maya glanced back briefly, catching a glimpse of Geeta, who mirrored Sid's mother's movements, her school bag swaying gently as she walked. Maya tightened her grip on her tabeez, her resolve hardening as the jungle seemed to close in around them.

They pressed on, deeper into the jungle, the air growing thicker and the shadows darker, as if the forest itself were preparing for what lay ahead.

The Plunge of Faith

"Who in the world am I? Ah, that's the great puzzle."

– Alice in the wonderland

Maruti took one last look at Vikram—or what remained of him. The skeleton rested within the hollow of a massive tree trunk, resembling a hideous throne. Vines coiled around the bony frame, while the skull was unnaturally elevated, suspended four or five feet above its neck by fungal stalks that spiraled upward like twisted sculptures. Mushrooms of vibrant hues erupted from the ribcage and limbs, their spores glinting faintly in the dim light. Tiny, twitching creatures skittered across the bones, weaving in and out, adding to the macabre scene.

Swati and Raosaheb stood near the source, silent sentinels. They could sense it—the approaching threat. It was armed. It was resolute.

Maruti's perception of the world had shifted entirely. The landscape blurred and twisted, as though viewed through a disturbed thermal lens—wavering, fragmented, and unreal. He could almost see sound, taste decay, and feel the musky scent of rot. His senses had merged into a chaotic, synesthetic nightmare, each one amplifying the other in unnatural harmony.

He no longer had eyes, only hollow sockets from which thick fungal stalks protruded. One eye dangled loosely near the shredded remains of his nose, its cloudy surface reflecting nothing. The skin on his face hung in tatters, stretched over deformed bones, riddled with oozing pores. No blood flowed from his decayed flesh—only a slimy, translucent residue born of fungal invasion.

Maruti wasn't dying. He was transforming. The ancient life growing within him was erasing his humanity, piece by piece. His thoughts, once his own, were now alien—primal, consumed by the source's singular purpose: protect, spread, survive.

Yet, there was no pain. Only maddening pleasure. It coursed through his body like an electric current, overwhelming, relentless. A low, guttural moan escaped his lips, vibrating through the oppressive jungle air.

Turning his head slowly, the fungal stalks sprouting from his skull swayed with the motion. He glanced at Swati and Raosaheb one final time. They stood unyielding, their fungal-infested forms as still and unrelenting as the jungle itself, guarding the source. Vikram.

Maruti began to crawl, dragging his grotesque body away from the clearing. His left leg hung uselessly, a decayed limb leaving behind faint trails of fungal slime. His clawed hands dug into the earth, pulling him forward inch by inch.

Away from the source. Away from danger.

The mushrooms whispered louder, urging him onward. Their collective will demanded he find untouched soil, new ground for their spores to thrive. They promised him purpose, a legacy of unending growth.

The jungle seemed to part for him, its shadows enveloping his malformed body as he disappeared deeper into its dark embrace. Behind him, Swati and Raosaheb remained steadfast at the source, their minds inextricably linked to the ancient fungus.

Maruti's progress was slow, his movements laborious. Each pull of his body left a faint, glistening trail of slime across the jungle floor. His limbs jerked unnaturally, controlled by the pulsating fungal growths that had consumed him entirely.

Then, abruptly, he stopped.

A guttural moan tore through the stillness, rising into a high-pitched shrill that echoed across the jungle, silencing even the insects. Maruti's head tilted upward, his neck trembling as the sound reverberated from deep within his decaying chest.

From the large mushrooms protruding from his hollow eye sockets, tiny pores ruptured with a sickening pop, releasing a cloud of shimmering spores. The particles floated into the air, catching the faint rays of sunlight piercing the dense canopy above.

Maruti twitched violently, his body convulsing as more jets of spores erupted from the fungal growths covering his torso and limbs. His movements were erratic, a grotesque dance of decay, until he finally managed to stand upright for the first time in hours. His head wobbled unnaturally, the jerking motion releasing more of the glittering particles into the air. The spores began to swirl, forming a mesmerizing, iridescent mist.

The pheromones.

The air around him glimmered, alive with the microscopic invaders carried by the gentle breeze that wound through the jungle. The spores danced as if with purpose, gliding effortlessly, their faint shimmer creating an almost magical spectacle. Yet, beneath the beauty lay something far more sinister. The jungle seemed to hold its breath, as if aware of the infection spreading through its veins.

Maruti let out another moan, softer this time, almost content. The pleasure coursing through his altered body reached its peak, a constant hum of satisfaction that overpowered any semblance of humanity left within him. Slowly, he turned his head, sniffing the air, his senses now a twisted blend of instinct and fungal control, attuned to the forest's unseen signals.

Then he moved again, deeper into the jungle. Each step was more deliberate, his malformed body dragging forward with purpose. He was no longer fleeing from the source—he was becoming one with it.

Behind him, the spores hung in the air, shimmering like stardust. Carried by the wind, they began their slow, silent creep toward the unsuspecting reaches of the forest.

The infection was spreading, a glimmering tide of doom creeping inexorably toward the rest of the world.

Bhairav ran through the jungle, his machete gripped tightly in one hand, the sacred dirt in the other. Guided by the presence of the Goddess—or something he couldn't quite name—he moved with uncanny certainty. There was no need for hallucinations or questioning; he simply knew where to go. Whether it was divine intervention, instinct, some buried primal urge, or the pheromones saturating the jungle air, he felt it coursing through him, driving him forward.

The jungle seemed alive, opening and closing around him as he moved. Towering trees swayed gently in the breeze, their shadows stretching long in the dimming light. The air grew thick, heavy with the cloying scent of damp earth and decay. His breaths were fast, shallow, but his resolve remained unshaken.

And then he stopped.

A sharp, undeniable pull tugged at his mind. The path ahead split in two. One fork led toward the direction he had been heading—familiar, distant, and weak. The other was closer, vibrant, and alive. It pulsed with energy, like the rhythmic beat of a heart reverberating through the trees.

Bhairav's chest heaved as he stood frozen at the fork, his body trembling with indecision. The new path called to him with a visceral urgency, its presence almost magnetic. It wasn't just a path; it was alive, and it wanted him to follow.

"Goddess, what should I do?" he whispered under his breath, his voice barely audible over the rustling of the leaves. His eyes darted between the two paths, uncertainty gnawing at the edges of his resolve.

The pull of the new path intensified, burrowing into his mind. It was no longer a choice—it was a compulsion, an ache that demanded to be answered. His hesitation melted away as he turned abruptly toward the unknown, his feet pounding against the forest floor.

The jungle shifted as he moved, its once-familiar embrace morphing into something sinister. The air grew denser, almost suffocating, and the shadows thickened, closing in from all sides. The pull strengthened, as if invisible hands were guiding him toward something waiting in the dark.

The machete in his hand felt heavier now, almost alive, its weight amplifying his sense of foreboding.

Bhairav pushed forward, his thoughts racing. *This isn't the Goddess… is it?* The flicker of doubt was brief but sharp, slicing through his certainty. Whatever this was, it was real. It was powerful.

And it left him no choice but to follow.

Maruti dragged his decaying body to the edge of the cliff, each movement slow and deliberate, his muscles twitching under the strain. The colorful particles radiating from his fungal-infested form shimmered in the dimming sunlight, drifting into the air like a toxic aurora. He paused at the precipice, the vast expanse of the jungle stretching endlessly behind him, and looked down.

The deep valley below was cloaked in mist, the faint roar of the river rising like a haunting melody of inevitability. The sound wasn't merely heard—it was felt, a vibration resonating through his malformed body. His muscles spasmed, his limbs trembling with exhaustion. He was reaching his limit, his grotesque form teetering on the edge of collapse.

This was the moment.

The whispers in his mind urged him forward. If he could make one final leap, the river would carry him far, far away— beyond the reach of those who sought to destroy him, to a new place where the ancient life within him could grow, thrive, and spread.

Behind him, the sound of footsteps. Bhairav burst through the dense foliage, his breathing labored, his machete gripped tightly in one hand. He stopped abruptly, his eyes widening as he took in the scene before him.

And then he felt it.

The presence of the Goddess washed over him like a wave, undeniable and all-consuming. His gaze shifted to the cliff's edge, where she stood, her towering figure framed by the golden light of the setting sun. Her arms were outstretched, her voice resonating with divine warmth.

"Come, my child! Come!" she beckoned, her tone a melody of reassurance and command.

Bhairav's machete slipped from his hand and fell to the ground with a dull thud. Tears streamed down his face as he stumbled forward, his body trembling. "Mother…" he whispered, his voice breaking.

He ran to her, collapsing into her embrace, his arms wrapping tightly around her. His tears fell freely, soaking into the folds of her ethereal presence. This was the moment he had prayed for, longed for—acceptance, forgiveness, and purpose.

But something was wrong.

The warmth he expected didn't come. Instead, his body was met with a cold, slimy wetness. He pulled back slightly, his vision clearing.

It wasn't the Goddess he was holding.

It was Maruti.

The fungal stalks protruding from Maruti's body oozed white goo, the sticky substance smearing across Bhairav's arms and chest. Maruti's hideous form shuddered violently, his remaining muscles spasming in one final, desperate effort.

Bhairav tried to push away, but Maruti convulsed, and a sudden burst of the white goo splattered across Bhairav's face. Some of it landed on his lips, and before he could react, it slipped into his open mouth.

Bhairav gagged, the taste bitter and metallic, his body recoiling in disgust. He clawed at his face, but the goo was already spreading, its insidious presence seeping into him.

With a guttural moan, Maruti lunged forward, his arms locking around Bhairav in a death grip. The momentum carried them both over the edge of the cliff.

Bhairav screamed, his voice echoing as they plummeted. The wind roared in his ears, the valley below rushing up to meet them. Maruti's body convulsed again, releasing another burst of shimmering particles into the air as they fell.

The river swallowed them whole, its dark, churning waters erasing their forms in an instant. But the infection had already begun its insidious work, taking root within Bhairav as the spores carried by the current promised to spread further.

The jungle fell silent, the only sound remaining the distant roar of the river, as if the forest itself was holding its breath.

The Last Stand

"Do not go gentle into that good night.
Rage, rage against the dying of the light."

– Dylan Thomas

"Shhhh," Sid signaled, crouching behind a thick tree trunk. His finger pressed to his lips as he pointed ahead. Maya and Baburao followed his gaze.

Swati and Raosaheb stood a short distance away, their bodies partially obscured by the dense jungle foliage. They were unnervingly still, their heads twitching slightly as if listening to something unseen.

"Do you see them?" Sid whispered.

"Yes," Baburao replied, his voice barely audible. "They're real."

Sid slid the knife he had found near the car toward Maya, gesturing for her to take it. She hesitated for a moment, the blade feeling unnaturally heavy in her hands. Her heart thudded against her ribs, her grip tightening around the weapon as if it could anchor her fear.

Pulling out his Colt, Sid took aim, his eyes narrowing as he focused on Raosaheb. The man—no, the creature—was enormous. The mushrooms erupting from his skin had deformed his body, making him even more monstrous. Sid knew this would be no easy fight.

He glanced at Baburao, silently seeking approval. Baburao gave a quick, firm nod.

"BANG!"

The.38 round tore through the air and struck Raosaheb squarely in the stomach, passing cleanly through and exiting out the other side. The roar that followed wasn't human. It was guttural, primal—a sound that sent chills down their spines.

Swati reacted instantly, leaping into the jungle with a speed that defied logic, her movements a blur as she disappeared into the trees.

"BANG!"

Sid fired again, but Raosaheb dropped to all fours, dodging the shot with an unnatural agility. Before Sid could react, Raosaheb lunged, his massive body closing the distance in a heartbeat.

Maya gasped, stumbling backward, the knife trembling in her hands. Her mind raced, her grip frozen as she watched the hulking figure collide with Sid like a battering ram. The sheer force of it sent him sprawling to the ground, and they rolled in a violent tangle of limbs.

"*Do something!*" her mind screamed at her, but her body wouldn't move. She could only watch as Raosaheb, impossibly strong, hurled Sid like a ragdoll into the trunk of a tree.

Sid hit the bark with a sickening thud, his head snapping back as blood trickled down the back of his neck. Maya's breath caught in her throat as she saw him falter, his Colt shaking in his hand.

Raosaheb roared again, crouching low as he prepared for another attack. Maya's fingers twitched around the knife, her knuckles white. She wanted to scream, to charge, to do something.

Sid, dazed but focused, raised his Colt, his arm trembling but steady enough to aim.

As Raosaheb charged, Sid squeezed the trigger.

"BANG!"

The bullet hit its mark, piercing straight through Raosaheb's forehead. The creature collapsed mid-stride, his massive body crashing to the ground in a grotesque heap.

The jungle fell silent for a moment, the oppressive stillness pressing down on them.

Baburao stepped forward cautiously, his machete in hand. He leaned over Raosaheb's corpse, his face grim as he examined the twitching fungal growths still sprouting from the body.

"Don't take chances," he muttered, gripping the machete with both hands.

With a swift motion, Baburao drove the blade deep into Raosaheb's chest, twisting it for good measure. A burst of white goo oozed out, spreading across the ground like spoiled milk. The smell was sickly sweet, and Maya turned away, gagging.

"Is he… dead?" Maya asked, her voice shaky.

"He's not getting back up," Baburao replied, yanking the machete free with a wet squelch. He wiped the blade against his pant leg, his face pale but resolute.

Sid slumped against the tree, his breath coming in ragged gasps. "Thanks," he said weakly, his voice barely audible.

Sid struggled to stand, his body swaying as his vision blurred. His head throbbed, and the world around him spun in and out of focus. From the distance, he heard her voice again.

"Sid…"

He turned his head weakly, his mother's silhouette beckoning him from the shadows, her hand motioning for him to follow. "Mother…" he murmured, his voice fragile, laden with longing. He tried to take a step, his legs wobbling beneath him, but they buckled under his weight.

Before he could collapse, Baburao was there, grabbing him firmly by the shoulders. "Steady," Baburao said, his tone calm but commanding. Sid leaned heavily on him, each step an effort as they moved forward.

"Mother," Sid muttered again, his voice trailing off as dizziness overtook him.

Maya glanced back and quickly assessed the situation. Dropping her pack, she removed her shirt, revealing a snug-fitting T-shirt underneath. Without hesitation, she folded the shirt and tied it tightly around Sid's head to stem the flow of blood. The makeshift bandage quickly darkened as it absorbed the crimson stain.

Sid blinked at her, his lips curling into a weak smile. "Thanks," he whispered, his voice barely audible over the hum of the jungle.

Maya gave him a curt nod, her focus already back on the path ahead. Baburao adjusted his grip on Sid, urging him to keep moving.

Sid's fingers trembled as he reached for the Colt holstered at his side. Its weight felt like a lead anchor dragging him down. With a groan of effort, he unlatched it and let it fall to the ground. The gun landed with a dull thud, empty and useless.

"I can't…" Sid started to say, but his words slurred as his body gave out. His legs folded beneath him, and his consciousness slipped away.

Baburao caught him just in time, easing him to the ground. "Maya, help me!" he barked, his voice sharp as he knelt beside Sid's limp form.

"We need to get help," Maya whispered, her voice trembling but resolute as she glanced at Sid's unconscious body.

"It's night. We can't leave him here," Baburao replied gruffly, his eyes scanning the shadows for any movement.

"He may die like this!" Maya's voice cracked, her frustration spilling over as she gestured to Sid, his makeshift bandage soaked through with blood.

Baburao didn't answer immediately. He crouched low, his machete resting against his leg, his expression grim. They had all taken the risk. They had all known the dangers. And yet, they had come—for a purpose that now felt maddeningly close, just out of reach.

Carrying Sid back to the village was impossible. The jungle would never let them move fast enough. But leaving him here wasn't an option either. The thought of Swati, somewhere in the dense foliage, watching them, sent a shiver down Baburao's spine.

And Swati was watching.

From a tree above them, her glowing eyes tracked their every movement. Her inhuman body, contorted and still, blended seamlessly with the shadows. Her gaze locked onto Sid first, his vulnerability drawing her. But then her attention shifted to Maya and Baburao. They were still armed, still dangerous.

The remnants of her human brain screamed, *Stop! Ask for help!* But it was nothing more than a faint echo in the void—a powerless whisper drowned by the dominant force of the fungus within her.

Her body moved without her will, gliding silently down the trunk of the tree. Her once-human hands, now twisted and clawed, dug into the bark as she descended, her movements eerily fluid.

Baburao froze, his ears catching the faint scrape of her claws against the wood. He gripped his machete tightly, his knuckles whitening as he scanned the darkness. "She's here," he muttered.

Maya's breath hitched, her grip tightening on the knife. The jungle around them seemed to close in, the sounds of the night amplifying every heartbeat, every rustle of leaves.

Swati emerged from the shadows, crawling low to the ground like a predator. Her dress hung in tatters, revealing patches of skin overtaken by fungal growths. Her once-beautiful face was now a mutilated mix of humanity and decay, her eyes glowing faintly in the darkness.

Maya and Baburao turned to face her.

The Colt lay on the ground beside Sid, empty and useless.

Maya's fingers trembled around the knife, her pulse hammering in her ears. Baburao raised his machete, his stance wide and firm.

Swati moved in a slow, deliberate circle around them, her body low and predatory. Her glowing eyes never left them, calculating, testing their reactions.

"Stay back," Baburao growled, his voice steady despite the fear creeping into his veins. He swung the machete in a wide arc, the blade catching a faint glint of moonlight.

Swati hissed, the sound more animal than human. Her movements quickened, her circle tightening as she probed for weakness.

Maya's chest heaved as she tried to focus, her knife shaking in her grip. "She's not stopping," she whispered.

"She's waiting," Baburao replied grimly. "Looking for an opening."

The tension was suffocating. Every second felt like an eternity as Swati continued her predatory dance. The jungle seemed to watch with bated breath, the distant cries of animals eerily absent.

Sid stirred faintly on the ground, a weak groan escaping his lips.

Swati's head snapped toward him instantly, her body lowering even further as if preparing to pounce.

Baburao stepped in front of Sid, machete raised high. "You'll have to go through me first," he said, his voice low and firm.

Swati paused, her glowing eyes narrowing. For a brief moment, the faintest flicker of humanity passed through her gaze. But it was gone in an instant, swallowed by the fungal force that drove her.

Maya took a step forward, the knife steady now in her hand. "We're not letting you take him," she said, her voice hard.

Swati hissed again, louder this time, the sound reverberating through the jungle. She crouched, her muscles coiling like a spring.

"Get ready," Baburao muttered, his eyes never leaving her.

Swati leaped like a cheetah, her movements swift and precise. Baburao reacted instinctively, swinging his machete with all his strength. The blade sliced across her stomach, releasing a gush of blood, but it wasn't enough to stop her.

She roared in rage, her strength undiminished, and lunged at him. Baburao barely had time to brace himself before she slammed into him, throwing him to the ground with terrifying force. His machete flew from his grasp, landing a few feet away.

Pinned beneath her, Baburao met her glowing, inhuman eyes. There was no trace of the Swati they had come to rescue— only a predator, cold and unrelenting. She ignored Maya entirely, her focus singular. Her hands clamped around Baburao's neck, her grip like iron.

Baburao's legs thrashed against the forest floor as he fought for air, his strength fading fast. Swati's grip tightened, her claws digging into his skin.

"Damn it. I need to do something. I need to…" Maya's thoughts raced, her hands trembling as she clutched the knife. Fear froze her in place for a moment, but then she moved.

With a sudden burst of courage, she lunged forward.

"SLUK!"

The knife drove into the back of Swati's neck, the blade piercing clean through to the front. Swati's body jerked violently, a guttural hiss escaping her throat as blood and fungal spores spattered the ground.

Maya yanked the knife free, her breaths ragged, and Swati slumped forward, collapsing onto Baburao.

Baburao groaned, shoving her lifeless body to the side. He coughed, sucking in deep breaths as he struggled to sit up. His leg twisted awkwardly beneath him, but he was alive.

He grabbed his machete from the ground, his face grim, and without hesitation drove the blade into Swati's chest. The sound was wet and sickening as it pierced her heart.

Maya, standing over them, trembled uncontrollably. Her hands shook, and the knife she had wielded fell to the ground. She stared at Swati's body, watching the last flickers of life leave her as faint gargling sounds escaped her throat.

She had killed. Not just a human—no, whatever Swati had become was far from that—but still, the act was overwhelming. She had never harmed so much as a fly before this moment, and now blood coated her hands.

"She's dead," Baburao said, his voice thick with emotion. He turned to Sid, kneeling beside him and pressing two fingers to his neck. Sid's eyes fluttered open, his breath shallow and ragged.

"But… I was supposed to be the lead," Sid rasped, a faint, bitter smile tugging at his lips. His gaze shifted to Baburao, his humor flickering through the pain.

"Old man… you're the side…"

His trembling fingers fumbled into his pocket, pulling out his wallet.

With unsteady hands, he pried it open and took a long, lingering look at the picture of Kavita.

"She was the heroine…" His voice cracked, barely above a whisper. "This can't be… I was going to get married."

His eyes moved to Maya.

His lips parted, as if to say something more—something important.

"And Maya…"

His voice faltered.

The words hung unfinished, suspended in the air as his breath hitched.

And then—silence.

His body stilled.

His eyes, once sharp with mischief, vacant.

Baburao froze.

His fingers pressed to Sid's neck.

His face darkened.

"No pulse."

Maya's breath hitched. The world blurred.

"What?" Her voice cracked, breaking apart as she stumbled forward. "No, no… he can't be…"

Her hands shook, reaching for him—but Sid was gone.

The universe, indifferent as ever, marched on. Throughout history, countless "leads"—heroes, dreamers, and do-gooders—must have met their premature ends, their stories left untold, their names forgotten. We only celebrate the ones who survive long enough to etch their names into memory, to bask in fleeting victories. For every legend remembered, countless others fade into obscurity, their struggles erased, their efforts swallowed by the vast, uncaring void.

The cosmos draws no lines between heroes and villains, the righteous and the wicked. It churns forward, unfeeling and relentless, blind to our triumphs and deaf to our cries.

In the end, survival isn't a reward—it's a coincidence. A cruel lottery where luck is often the only thing that separates the remembered from the forgotten.

Tears welled in Baburao's eyes as he pressed his fingers harder against Sid's neck, searching desperately for any sign of life. His expression fell further as realization set in. "He's gone."

Maya shook her head, stepping closer. "No, no…" She knelt beside Sid, her trembling hands hovering above his still chest as if willing him to breathe. "Sid, wake up!" Her voice cracked, the desperation raw and unrestrained.

Baburao placed a firm hand on her shoulder. "It's too late," he said softly, his voice heavy with sorrow.

Maya stared at Sid's pale face, her mind screaming for a solution, anything to undo what had happened. But his lifeless form offered no response. Tears blurred her vision as she clutched his limp hand, the warmth already fading.

"We need to move," Baburao said after a long pause, his tone firm but subdued. "Staying here will only make us targets."

Maya didn't move. She couldn't. The weight of her grief rooted her to the spot, her fingers gripping Sid's hand as if letting go would mean accepting the truth.

Baburao crouched beside her, his voice softening. "I know this hurts, but if we don't leave now, we're dead too. Sid wouldn't want us to die here."

His words broke through her fog of despair. With a shaky breath, Maya nodded, releasing Sid's hand reluctantly. Her heart ached with every step she took away from him, the image of his still body burned into her mind.

Baburao adjusted his machete, his expression grim. "We'll come back for him. Once this is over… we'll bring him home."

Maya swallowed hard, her grip tightening on her tabeez. "We have to stop this. Whatever it takes," she said, her voice trembling but resolute.

"I can't walk properly," Baburao admitted, his leg dragging awkwardly beneath him as he tried to stand.

"Lean on me," Maya said, slipping her arm under his shoulder.

"Where do we go?" Baburao asked, his voice laced with frustration. "Sid was our guide. Without him…"

"I have a guide too," Maya interrupted, her voice steady despite her trembling.

Baburao turned to her in confusion. She was looking into the distance, her eyes focused on something unseen.

There, among the shadows of the jungle, stood Geeta. The little girl in her school dress waved at Maya, her innocent smile urging her forward.

"You're seeing something, aren't you?" Baburao asked, his tone careful, tinged with concern.

Maya nodded, refusing to meet his gaze. "Let's move. Trust me."

Baburao hesitated, his eyes narrowing, but he didn't question her. They followed Maya's unseen guide deeper into the jungle.

They didn't have to walk much. Just a few paces into the dense jungle, and Geeta came into view again. She sat on the trunk of a massive tree, her school dress as neat and vibrant as Maya remembered.

"Why don't you come here, Maya?" Geeta's voice was sweet, melodic, and unnervingly familiar. She extended her small hand, a brightly wrapped candy resting on her palm. "Come and take this candy. You used to love it."

Maya took a hesitant step forward, her legs moving almost involuntarily. There was something magnetic about Geeta's voice, a pull that defied logic.

But before she could get any closer, Baburao's firm grip yanked her back.

"Stop!" he hissed, his voice trembling.

"What?" Maya snapped, twisting to look at him.

"Can't you see?" Baburao's face was pale, his wide eyes fixed on the tree.

"See what?" Maya demanded, glancing back at Geeta. The little girl smiled sweetly, her hand still outstretched.

"It's… it's…" Baburao stammered, his voice breaking as he pointed. Maya followed his gaze and froze.

What she saw wasn't Geeta.

The tree was massive, its gnarled roots twisted and claw-like, anchoring it firmly into the damp earth. Perched on its trunk was a grotesque sight: a skeleton, half-fused with the bark. The remains of a man sat like a king on a throne, his body overrun by vibrant, colorful mushrooms. His skull had stretched unnaturally high, as if pulled by unseen forces, while crawlers slithered through his ribcage.

The GoPro was still attached to his skull, now claimed by moss and decay. The tiny device, long dead, had lost its blinking red eye, its battery drained to nothing. Yet, time had not erased everything. Inside, nestled within the lifeless shell, the SD card remained untouched—silent, hidden, preserving Vikram's final moments. The jungle had consumed his body, but within that tiny, forgotten relic, his last breath, his final gaze, and the horrors he witnessed still lingered, waiting to be unearthed.

"Vikram…" Baburao whispered, his voice trembling with dread. "It's him. The source."

Maya's breath hitched. Her vision wavered, flickering between the smiling image of Geeta and the horrifying reality of Vikram's skeletal remains.

"Don't go near it," Baburao warned, his grip tightening on her arm. "It will infect you."

Maya struggled against his hold, her breath coming in short, uneven gasps.

She saw only Geeta.

The little girl tilted her head, her voice soft, lilting, yet laced with something unnatural.

"You loved candy, didn't you, Maya?"

A pause. A knowing, playful smirk.

"Or… do you want a kiss?"

Geeta's lips parted, slow, deliberate—too deliberate.

A shiver rippled through Maya, her stomach twisting.

This isn't real. It can't be real.

She blinked rapidly, her vision swimming, her grip on the tabeez tightening until her knuckles turned white.

She murmured a prayer, the words tumbling out in a breathless whisper, as if sheer force of will could shatter the illusion.

Her mind fought to reconcile the impossible.

But Geeta was still there.

Still smiling.

And Maya was still trembling.

"Geeta's not real," she whispered to herself, forcing her feet to take a step back.

The vision of Geeta wavered, her innocent smile twisting into something far more sinister.

"I'm not falling for this," Maya said firmly, retreating further.

Baburao exhaled in relief, his shoulders relaxing slightly. "Good. Now we need to leave."

"And do what?" Maya asked, her voice shaky but regaining strength.

"We go to the authorities," Baburao said, gripping his machete tightly. "We tell them everything. They'll have to burn this place down. That's the only way to end this."

Maya nodded, her eyes lingering on the gnarled figure fused to the tree. The colorful mushrooms pulsated faintly, as if alive, and a strange, low hum seemed to emanate from the trunk. She shuddered.

As they turned to leave, the jungle seemed to exhale, the faint glitter of spores catching the moonlight. Maya hesitated, glancing back. Was it her imagination, or had the skeletal remains shifted slightly, its hand raised as if to reach out?

"Let's go," Baburao urged, his voice firm but low. As they turned to leave.

"Maya, don't leave me here!"

The voice stopped her cold.

Geeta's voice. Small. Trembling. Familiar.

Maya turned sharply. The jungle twisted with shadows, but there, near the base of the tree, something moved.

"We'll have candies together," Geeta pleaded. Her voice cracked, raw with despair.

Maya's breath caught in her throat. She could see Geetha's delicate frame half-buried in the tree's bark.

Baburao gripped Maya's arm. "It's playing with you," he muttered, his voice tight.

Maya's vision blurred. Tears streamed down her face. The weight of Geetha's small hand in hers, the echo of their shared laughter—Hindi lessons after school, the scribbled notes on Maya's notebook, the way Geetha always stole extra chocolates from her lunchbox—memories crashed over her like a tidal wave.

"Please… Maya… remember our Hindi class…"

A sob. Then a scream. Then raw, broken pleading.

Maya turned away.

She walked. Baburao leaning on her for support.

They began to walk away, their footsteps muffled by the damp earth. The jungle closed in behind them, its oppressive silence broken only by the faint rustling of leaves.

Maya clutched her tabeez, her grip tight. The image of Geeta's innocent face lingered in her mind, but so did the freakish reality of Vikram's remains. She tried to shake the thought but couldn't help wondering—*was this truly over, or had they just seen the beginning of something far worse?*

As they walked, her thoughts unraveled like loose threads. The jungle surrounded her—ancient trees stretching endlessly into the night, gnarled roots twisting beneath her feet, insects half-buried in the moist soil, their small, fragile lives blinking in and out of existence.

Baburao's voice echoed in her mind.

"Burn it down!"

Should we?

The question gnawed at her. *Was this place an aberration, a mistake of nature? Or was it simply the next inevitable step in evolution? Who were they to decide—to destroy it or to accept that perhaps, it was their time to disappear instead?*

And then there was Geeta.

"Burn it down!"

The words clashed against her thoughts, against the whispering shadows pressing in from all sides. She felt the weight of them, their finality.

Maya exhaled sharply and kept walking.

She didn't have an answer. Not yet. And she kept walking…

The Aftermath

"The woods are dark, their roots run deep, and buried secrets never sleep."

– Anonymous

Maya sat on the edge of the sterile cot, her eyes fixed on the flickering television screen mounted on the whitewashed wall of her quarantine room. The news anchor's voice was calm, detached, recounting the story of the massive fire that had engulfed Khandav for the last two weeks. Aerial footage filled the screen, showing blackened earth—a wasteland stretching endlessly beneath the camera's gaze.

The chyron read: *"Uncontrolled Forest Fire Devastates Region— Evacuations Underway."*

Maya's jaw tightened. She knew better. This wasn't a natural disaster—it was a calculated act, a cleansing. The government had ensured that no trace of Khandav's ecosystem survived. Fifty kilometers of jungle, villages, and wildlife—all reduced to ash. Dongarwadi and neighboring villages had been evacuated under the pretense of fire hazards, but the truth was far darker.

The burning wasn't just about containment; it was an offering, a sacrifice to rid the world of something ancient and uncontrollable. Security forces armed with guns and flamethrowers had surrounded the inferno, ensuring that any escaping animals or insects were incinerated. Khandav was once more offered to the fire god, Agni. But this time, it was not Arjuna and Krishna slaughtering the innocent creatures as they fled the inferno. The military had taken their place. The state had descended with full force, its will absolute, its judgment final. Not a single grasshopper, not a single bird was meant to leave the scorched ground alive.

The jungle writhed as it burned, the night filled with a symphony of dying echoes.

But fire was never the end.

It was only the beginning.

Before the flames were lit, the government had collected samples—soil, spores, and blood. She remembered the hazmat suits, the eerie silence as they scoured the jungle floor. The scientists whispered of ancient DNA, of potential breakthroughs in medicine, and, more ominously, of weapons.

Maya glanced down at the needle marks dotting her arms—the result of three relentless weeks of blood draws and medical tests. They hadn't been looking for diseases. They were searching for secrets. She'd overheard snippets of conversations: *"Mutagenic potential… hallucinogenic compounds… behavioral control."*

She shuddered, recalling the mention of an ancient recipe, something connected to Chendkai's father—a drink to enslave, to control. It wasn't just about erasing Khandav. It was about harnessing it.

Her thoughts drifted to Siddharth, his bloodied face flashing in her mind. She could still hear his voice, steady even in the chaos, urging them forward. The memory of his lifeless body in the jungle made her chest tighten.

"They'll say he died in the fire," Baburao had muttered when they first entered quarantine. "They'll erase him, just like they'll erase everything else."

Maya had nodded, her throat tight. "But we'll remember. That has to be enough."

The television droned on, but Maya tuned it out, her mind consumed by those last moments. Siddharth deserved better. They all did.

A knock at the door broke her reverie. It swung open, and a middle-aged man in a crisp white suit stepped in, clipboard in hand. His expression was unreadable.

"Congratulations," he said flatly. "You're free to go."

Maya blinked, unsure whether to feel relief or suspicion. She stood and stepped into the brightly lit corridor, where Baburao was already waiting, his expression grim.

"Three weeks of needles and locked doors, and this is how it ends?" Baburao muttered as she joined him.

They were escorted down the hall, their every step echoing against the polished floors. At the exit, a suited government official awaited them, his smile as polished as his shoes.

"Ms. Maya, Mr. Baburao, I'm here to thank you on behalf of the government," he began smoothly. "Your cooperation has been invaluable. Now, as we've discussed, your old lives are behind you. Forget what you've seen. Forget what you've done. This is your fresh start."

Maya and Baburao exchanged a wary glance.

"You've been cleared to leave quarantine," the man continued, gesturing toward a sleek black car waiting outside. "Come with us. We'll take care of you. New jobs, new identities—no loose ends."

Maya hesitated. "And what about Siddharth?" she asked, her voice sharper than she intended.

The man's polished smile faltered for a fraction of a second before returning. "Mr. Siddharth's… contributions are deeply appreciated. He will be remembered."

Maya's stomach churned. *Remembered? By whom?* She knew the truth—Siddharth's name would never see the light of day.

"He's dead because of this," she said, her voice breaking.

"And you're alive," the man replied coolly. "Because of him. That's what matters now."

Baburao placed a hand on her shoulder, a silent gesture to let it go. Maya bit her lip, anger simmering beneath the surface, and followed him out.

Behind them, the facility door clicked shut, sealing away the remnants of Khandav's nightmare.

As Maya climbed into the car, her mind raced. Should she go to the press? People needed to know. The story had to be told—Siddharth's sacrifice deserved more than silence. *But who would print it?* The government had everything under control. If she spoke out, her words would be dismissed as conspiracy theories, scattered across unverified YouTube channels and lost in the void of unauthenticated chatter.

The car began to move, its smooth hum a stark contrast to the chaos that raged in her thoughts.

Maya stared out the window, her resolve wavering. Behind her, Khandav was gone. Ahead of her, the government's shadow loomed. All she could do now was wonder—and decide.

And then there was Nasreen.

The only person, since Geeta, Maya truly felt anything for. The only tether to a world that still made sense.

She exhaled, her fingers tightening around her phone as she dialed. The first ring barely passed before Nasreen's voice burst through, frantic and breathless.

"Maya? Where the hell have you been? We tried calling you so many times! Oh God… did you see the news? Are you okay? The jungle—it's burning! Where are you?"

Maya opened her mouth to respond, but Nasreen didn't stop.

"Ma was worried sick. She must have called me a hundred times! Your phone was out of range for days, and then switched off! Maya, what happened? I swear, I'm coming to get you, just tell me where—"

Maya closed her eyes, and for a moment, she wasn't in the car anymore. She was with Nasreen, watching her talk, watching the way her pink lips moved—fast, barely pausing for breath. The way her delicate fingers curled as she gestured, even when no one was looking. The way her dark, expressive eyes flickered between worry and frustration, the faint crease between her brows deepening with every question.

Maya could see her. Could almost reach out and touch the warmth of her pale skin, the familiar scent of rosewater lingering in the air between them.

But Nasreen was not here. And Maya was no longer the person she had been before the jungle.

"Nasreen—"

The words caught in her throat, but Nasreen barely heard her. The flood of worry, frustration, and relief continued.

Maya exhaled sharply, gripping the phone tighter. A lump formed in her chest, the weight of everything pressing down. She had survived. But for what? What was left of her now?

"NASREEN!"

The name ripped from her lungs, silencing the storm on the other end. For a moment, there was only breathing. A pause thick with something neither of them could name.

Then, Maya whispered, voice raw, stripped bare.

"I love you."

Whispers from Underground

"That is not dead which can eternal lie,

And with strange aeons even death may die."

– H.P. Lovecraft

Around 200 kilometers from Khandav, deep in the heart of Karnataka, the sun hung low on the horizon, casting long shadows over the outskirts of a quiet village. The air buzzed with the rhythmic drone of cicadas, blending with the excited shouts of boys playing cricket in a dusty clearing.

"Six!" one of them shouted as the ball soared high, past the road, and into the edge of the woods.

"Sonya, get it!" another boy called out, pointing toward the dense foliage where the ball had disappeared.

Sonya, a wiry fifteen-year-old with quick reflexes, dashed after it. His bare feet kicked up plumes of dust as he sprinted across the uneven ground, his focus fixed on the trees. He stopped at the edge of the woods, peering into the shadows.

The ball had rolled farther than expected, disappearing into the underbrush. He hesitated, his fingers brushing against the bark of a nearby tree. The woods seemed unnaturally quiet, the fading sunlight barely penetrating the dense canopy.

Something shimmered faintly in the air—glittering particles that caught the light like dust motes in a sunbeam. Sonya wrinkled his nose at a faint, earthy smell, both sweet and cloying, hanging heavy in the still air. He waved a hand in front of his face, trying to dispel the scent, but it clung stubbornly, making his stomach turn.

"Sonya!"

The voice froze him in place. It was familiar, warm. He turned sharply, his wide eyes scanning the shadows.

There, just beyond the first line of trees, stood his grandfather.

Sonya's breath caught in his throat. His grandfather had passed away six months ago, but here he was, standing as clear as day. His kind face was framed by neatly combed white hair, and he wore his usual white dhoti and kurta. His weathered hands were clasped gently behind his back, just as Sonya remembered.

"*Ajja?*" Sonya whispered, his voice trembling.

The other boys' shouts faded into the background, distant and unimportant. His grandfather smiled warmly, nodding slightly.

"Come, Sonya," the old man said gently. "Come here, my boy."

Sonya hesitated, his heart pounding in his chest. His mind screamed at him to run back to the safety of the field, but his feet remained rooted to the spot. The pull was irresistible.

"*Ajja,*" he whispered again, taking a cautious step forward. His hands trembled as he moved closer, the underbrush crunching softly beneath his feet.

"Don't be afraid," his grandfather said, his voice soft and familiar. He beckoned with one hand, stepping deeper into the woods.

The cricket bat slipped from Sonya's hand, falling silently onto the dusty ground. He stepped past the edge of the woods, following the figure deeper into the trees.

The air around him seemed to hum, the glittering particles thickening as he walked. The strange, earthy smell grew sharper, pricking at his senses. Somewhere in the distance, the faint sound of running water whispered through the jungle, a reminder of the river that passed near the village.

The shadows swallowed him whole, the laughter of his friends fading entirely.

"*Ajja*, wait for me!" Sonya called, his voice carrying into the dense stillness of the forest.

And then, there was silence.

A kilometer away, near the flowing river, a grotesque sight awaited. The skeletal remains of the Bhairav sat entwined within the gnarled roots of a giant tree. From his decayed form sprouted large, bulbous mushrooms, their fleshy caps pulsating faintly, releasing a fine, glittering mist into the air.

The forest held its breath, watching, as the boy vanished into its depths.

* * *